S0-ABD-171

The Secrets of Hidden Creek

The Secrets of

Illustrated by Paul Galdone

Hidden Creek

Wylly Folk St. John

A CAMELOT BOOK/PUBLISHED BY AVON BOOKS

This book is for the real Becky and Jenny and Chuck:
the children I love, who love mysteries.

AVON BOOKS
A division of
The Hearst Corporation
959 Eighth Avenue
New York, New York 10019

Copyright © 1966 by Wylly Folk St. John
Published by arrangement with The Viking Press
Library of Congress Catalog Card Number: 66-10434

ISBN: 0-380-00746-0

All rights reserved, which includes the right
to reproduce this book or portions thereof in
any form whatsoever. For information address
The Viking Press, 625 Madison Avenue,
New York, N. Y. 10022

First Camelot Printing, August, 1976

CAMELOT TRADEMARK REG. U.S. PAT. OFF. AND IN
OTHER COUNTRIES, MARCA REGISTRADA, HECHO EN
U.S.A.

Printed in the U.S.A.

Contents

Other Camelot Books by
Wylly Folk St. John

THE SECRET OF THE SEVEN CROWS   26237 $1.25
THE SECRET OF THE PIRATE INN   28480 $1.25

WYLLY FOLK ST. JOHN is a true Southerner. She was born in South Carolina, spent her childhood in Savannah, graduated from the University of Georgia in Athens, and is now living in Social Circle, not far from Atlanta. She was employed as a staff writer for the Magazine Section of the *Atlanta Journal and Constitution* for many years.

Ghosts at Wormwood

Jenny and Chuck never get blamed for anything. I'm the one who always gets in trouble about everything we do. Mama says, "You're the oldest, Becky, and you ought to know better!" Maybe I do know better, usually —but sometimes you just have to take a chance.

It's not too good, being the oldest. There are a few advantages, I admit, but I think the others ought to take a little responsibility sometimes. It'd be good for them. They'll never get a turn at being the oldest—I'm stuck with it. I'm nearly fourteen—well, I will be next February—and Chuck's only seven, but Jenny's going-on-eleven and quite bright for her age. Of course she's had the advantage of rooming with me all her life.

I honestly don't think Chuck by himself would ever have thought of going ghost-hunting at Wormwood that night, but it should have been clear to Grandma that the whole thing was Jenny's idea, not mine. Jenny admitted it, and I had to give her the credit. But afterward Grandma said I should have said No, or else I should have come and asked, and then she could have been the one to say No. I bet she wouldn't have actually, though. Grandma sees our point of view pretty often, except when it's about something she thinks is really dangerous. Then she can be a real worry-wart. But we didn't think the ghost-hunt was dangerous—at the time, anyway.

The three of us were spending the whole summer with Grandma and Sarge. Our grandfather is a retired Army sergeant and for some reason he'd rather be called Sarge than Grandpa. They'd just bought a summer cabin in the Blue Ridge Mountains in North Georgia, for him to retire to, and they thought we'd enjoy spending our school vacation there. We did, too.

But you know how it is. The cabin was fun for about three days. We each had a tree-seat, where Jenny and I sat and read and Chuck pretended he was a bird chirping and twittering and sitting on eggs. Sarge helped us build a lean-to in the woods, and they let us have our own cookouts and roast potatoes in our campfire the way the Indians did, except we wrapped them in foil instead of in mud or corn shucks.

Sarge really tried to amuse us, I'll say that for him.

He put up a grand swing for us out by the barbecue pit. He let us take the boat out in the lake and swim from it, too, whenever he wasn't far away. And he showed Chuck how to bait our fishhooks. Chuck doesn't mind handling worms any more than Sarge does. Jenny and I wouldn't touch them for the world.

But after about three days we got pretty tired of doing the same old things. Grandma had written Mama to be sure to let us come while the lake was up, as she'd been told that the electric-power people would begin to draw the water down in July. They make electricity with it somehow, and control floods, though I'm not too sure how. Soon after the Fourth of July, our whole end of the lake would disappear until next spring, leaving just a valley where it had been. Grandma said she wanted us to be there while the lake was too, so that we could swim and fish, because she didn't know what she was going to do with us after that. Sarge could always have a good time working in his garden or taking the boat on his trailer to another lake to fish, and Grandma could have a good time picking blackberries and crab apples and making jelly and all, but she told Mama there weren't any organized activities for children up there. Mama wrote back for Grandma not to worry about that—we usually organized our own activities, but to be sure to keep a sharp eye on those, as they were generally way out. It's true we don't play paper-dolls exactly, and we do have pretty good fun when our Fine-Brain Club can think up something new to do. Like this scary idea of Jenny's.

Mama and Daddy weren't coming for us until Labor Day. It was only the last of June and we were already getting bored. At home we have plenty of friends. There's Mike—he asks me to the drive-in movie whenever his mama and dad take him. Jenny and her friend Thomas go rock-hunting on their bikes, and Chuck has a friend named John to play spies and Batman with. And there are Diane and Shay and Beverly and Karen—we can always find something to do with them. Here there was nobody to do anything with. The first day, I did see a boy with yellow hair at that old shack around the bend on the clay road that goes between the paved road and the cabin, but Grandma said she doubted if we'd like him.

He looked pretty clean, though, for a boy. His name was Arie Chance, she said, but his mother's name was Mrs. Strickland. I asked why, and she said, frankly, because his father was no good and his mother took back her maiden name when he got killed fighting with another man over a robbery. But Dorcy Strickland thought the children—she had four of them—had to have their father's name even if he did happen to be a criminal. If they didn't, some of their teachers might have been even more confused about the home situation.

"You mean their father stole something?" Jenny asked in a shocked voice.

"Did he hold up a bank?" asked Chuck.

"No, he didn't hold up anybody," Grandma explained. "But people think—in fact it was practically proved—that he and another man stole a very valuable collection of rare gold coins minted not far from here in Dahlonega, Georgia, some of them before the California Gold Rush. The collection was worth nearly fifty thousand dollars as a whole, because there are only a few complete collections of these special coins in existence. Even individually, there's no telling how much they'd be worth to collectors. One coin was the 1861 gold dollar. Only about six of those have ever been found, and the last time anybody sold one, it brought nearly six thousand dollars."

"Looks like the robbers couldn't very well sell a collection like that without everybody knowing," I said.

"That's just it—they couldn't. They'd have had to hold it for years, until the search for them died down, and then sell the individual coins through some shady dealer, probably for less than they're worth. But still, it would seem like a lot of money to people like the Chances. Anyway, the stolen coins were never found, and the college over near Auraria that owned the collection is still offering a reward for any information about it."

"And the robbers got away with it?" I asked.

"One of them did. But J. D. Chance, Arie's father, was killed by his partner. Nobody knew whether he was killed accidentally or on purpose, but the other man disappeared with the coin collection and nobody's heard a word about him since. He's wanted for suspected murder, of course, as well as for stealing the rare coins."

"Poor Mrs. Strickland," Jenny said. "Poor Arie, and the rest of them. Are there any girls?" she asked Grandma.

"Yes, but the little girl's smaller than you and the older girl's much bigger than Becky. The little boy is younger than Chuck. About five, I guess. He was just a baby when it all happened."

"What're their names?"

"I believe the small girl is Bonnie and the big girl is Millie. The boys are Arie and Del. Or so people around here tell me. I've not met them yet myself. You can speak to them if you see them, of course, but don't go up to their house."

"Why not?" That was Chuck, always wanting to know.

"Because Mrs. Strickland sells something at that old shack—people go up there in cars all the time—and it may be moonshine liquor for all we know. Of course, she does have to make a living somehow for those four children, but I wish her customers wouldn't keep our road all torn up, driving in there when it's been raining, and cutting ruts in the mud."

"But it might be just eggs she sells," Jenny argued. "Then maybe they could be our friends."

"Oh, Jenny!" I said. "Honestly! We probably wouldn't like them at all."

So even if it is neat to have the Fine-Brain Club in the family, we were getting a little bored with ourselves that night when Jenny had her bright idea. We had just finished supper and were sitting on the porch over-looking the lake. It's beautiful there, with the sunset behind the mountains showing in the water. I painted a picture of it for Mama, and she said it was good. It had to be because the clouds were so lovely, all rosy and fiery.

We were squabbling about whose turn it was to have the hammock first. Grandma and Sarge had gone inside to watch TV because his nerves couldn't stand us any longer. Sarge never has caught on that we aren't really fussing. It just sounds that way to anybody listening. If we'd been really mad at each other, we wouldn't have been speaking, much less quarreling.

Twilight was just about over, and now there were purple banks of clouds—a storm might be coming up—and big thundery gray ones with gold edges. Then there was a streak of lightning, and Jenny said, "It looks like

14

a snake putting out its tongue." She saw a snake once and she thought it put out its tongue at her.

"It might rain," Chuck said. He doesn't like rain much. I kind of enjoy it myself.

"It might not," I told him.

"Then let's go over there," Jenny said, cutting her eyes across the lake at the ruins of the old mansion that stood between the mountains and the edge of the water. Jenny looks like a little imp sometimes, with her blonde hair standing up in wisps—Mama says it's a cowlick—and her eyes bright blue like the gas flame under a kettle, so blue you can hardly stand it. I wish I were as skinny as Jenny. She wouldn't have to worry about getting fat even if she ate fudge-cake all day long. "Mr. Burdett down at the store says that old house is haunted. We might get to see a real live ghost."

I felt prickles on the back of my neck. The place across the lake looked like something an author named Edgar Allan Poe wrote about in Grandma's book with the horrible pictures of ruined castles with bats, and people decaying and dribbling down the sides of their coffins. Grandma had heard that the name of the old mansion was Winwood, and she said that some dark Halloween-like night she would tell us all about it.

"I already know all about it," Jenny said complacently when I reminded her of Grandma's promise. "Mr. Burdett told me. And as for me, I'm calling it

Wormwood." Jenny's teacher Miss Morris says Jenny has a very original turn of phrase when it comes to naming things. She named the pony she rode on at the park Whoa-Boy, and her beagle puppy Bullet Louise Dodd. (I named mine Gift because Daddy gave him to me.) And Grandma is always telling people how when Jenny was just a baby and Mama asked her what color flower she wanted to pick the child said "Vanilla." I don't think that was so awfully cute, myself.

Now Chuck really is cute. Even Mama has to laugh at him. He thinks he's cussing when he says "Gee Wiggles!" and the way he says it, it actually almost sounds like bad language. We don't know where he got it, but I kind of suspect Jenny. She's the type who'd make up cuss words. She used to say, "Double-dog-gone!" herself, but she thinks she's too old to say it now. In fact, now that she's growing up, she even wants us to call her Jennifer. I'm afraid we don't remember very often though.

"Why you gonna call it that?" Chuck asked her now. "What's a wormwood?" He has light hair too, a crew cut like a trimmed-down hairbrush. I'm the dark one. I look like Daddy and the rest of the Dodds, and I'm glad, even though Mama is prettier.

Jenny pushed Chuck out of the hammock and plopped down in it herself. "Because it's a wormy kind of house, see, and it has lots of woods. And ghosts. And Wormwood sounds kind of like Winwood."

"You give me the hammock," I bargained, "and I'll let you tell us about it. Come on, Chuck, you can sit in it with me." Jenny used to fall for a deal like that when she was little, but not any more. We ended up all three sitting in it, as usual, sliding down on top of one another in the middle. I never do get to enjoy the hammock by myself.

"Well," Jenny said mysteriously, "there's an old lady like a witch who lives over there all by herself. Her name is Mrs. Beadle."

"Beetle? Mrs. Beetle?" Chuck squeaked as if he couldn't believe it. "Gee Wiggles!"

"Beadle, silly. Not like a bug. Beadle."

"Why?"

"Because it was her husband's name, I guess. Anyhow her great-great-granduncle came over here from England a long time ago."

"How long?"

"Lots of years, I guess. Mr. Burdett didn't know for sure, but he said it was prob'ly about 1820."

"That's a hundred and forty-six years ago, Chuck," I told him. "A real long time ago. Before the War between the States."

"Well, anyway," Jenny said impatiently, "he was named Jeff-er-ey Winslow, and he was the son of some English lord or something—but not the oldest son— and he wanted to build a castle like his daddy and granddaddy had had in England. Because he loved this pretty girl, see, and married her and brought her here, and they didn't have any nice place to live. So first he built a few rooms they could live in—that's where Mrs. Beadle lives now—and then he started on his castle, right next to it. He built another wing on the other side—that's where the ghosts live now. It has a roof too. Then he built the walls of the castle in the middle. He was going to join the wings onto it. He built the walls and the window holes and a chimney and two towers and some steps, but not the roof. His wife planted the garden with all kinds of trees and plants that old Jefferey brought over the sea from Europe—France and England—and all, and some of the trees have grown taller than the towers now. There's a marble lady from Italy in the middle, where he had a fountain, and there's a maze made out of boxwood. . . . What's a maze exactly, Becky?"

"What's boxwood?" Chuck put in.

"I think a maze is a kind of puzzle, maybe alleys between tall boxwood hedges—boxwood is a bush, Chuck—that you might get lost in if you don't know just where to turn to find the end of it."

"Well, she planted one, and you can get lost in it mighty easy now, Mr. Burdett says, because it's all overgrown with blackberry vines and honeysuckle. Only you won't, because Mrs. Beadle doesn't allow anybody to come on her place at all. She never even has any company. She makes the grocery boy leave the groceries by the mailbox out at the gate. And he peeked in and said the marble lady is lying on her side, all broken."

"Go on about the castle."

"It never got finished. Jefferey's wife died, and his heart was broken. He couldn't bear to finish it without her. So the roof wasn't ever put on. Mr. Burdett thinks maybe his money gave out, too. They had to stash all the beautiful furniture and pictures and gold clocks and things he had brought from Europe to furnish it with, in the wing where Mrs. Beadle lives now. She's had to sell lots of them for money to live on."

"What happened to Jefferey then?"

"He and his brother quarreled, and they had a poison duel with wine. Mrs. Beadle still has the wine glasses with the dregs of the old poison dried up in them. And Jefferey was the one who lost. He died from the duel, and his ghost haunts the ruins of the castle, with its walls falling in and trees growing up in the rooms and the stairs tumbling down. And his wife's ghost wanders around in the maze in a white dress, crying."

"Did they have any children?"

"No. His brother's family inherited the place, but they were Cursed, and all sorts of terrible things have happened to them ever since. The brother's son went to California and one day his ghost appeared to Mrs. Beadle's great-grandmother, and sure enough a telegram came to say he'd died that very same day. And her grandfather was killed right there in the garden during the War Between the States by a Yankee. He's buried where he fell, and sometimes you can see *his* ghost standing there in its gray uniform, bleeding all over everything. But when you look afterwards, there isn't any blood.

"And Mrs. Beadle's own son went out of his mind and killed his sister right there in her wing of the house, in her living room, and the bloodstains won't wash off the floor no matter what they scrub it with. He got sent to the mental hospital because he didn't know, of course, what he was doing to his poor sister. But Mr. Burdett says she hasn't turned into a ghost yet. That was only about thirty years ago."

"That's a mighty lot of old ghosts, all the same," Chuck said. "Do we believe in ghosts, Becky?"

"I'm not sure," I told him. My neck was prickling just as if I did believe in them, though.

"Well, I'd like to see one," Jenny said, being very daring because after all we were right there with her, and Grandma and Sarge were close by. "Then I'd know whether I believe in them or not. So let's go over there tonight."

"Tonight?" I said doubtfully. It did look like rain.

"This is just the kind of night for ghosts, I think."

The gold edges of the sunset had all gone now and the sky was getting darker and darker. The wind was coming across the lake and blowing the trees wildly, and it made a kind of howling noise. We could just barely see the water, and it was all ruffled up. In fact, we were going to have a real black night.

I couldn't let Jenny and Chuck think I was chicken —I'm the one who thought up the Fine-Brain Club. "All right," I said, "how do you plan to get over there, my dear little sister? We can't possibly walk that far around by the road, at night. We might step on a snake."

"Boat," Jenny said simply. "After they go to sleep."

I swallowed hard. "All right," I said again. We had never taken the boat all the way across the lake, but Sarge hadn't told us not to. He hadn't told us not to go out in it at night, even—or not to go to Wormwood. He just hadn't thought about giving us those particular orders; he had no idea what-all we could think of to do that a grandfather ought to tell us not to do. "But, Chuck, you'd better stay here. I promised Mama not to let anything happen to her baby boy."

"I," said Chuck, turning up his funny little snub nose, "promised Daddy to take care of you girls. If anybody goes, I'm going. Or I'll tell."

"Oh, let him go, Beck," Jenny urged.

"Well—" I finally agreed.

The sleeping porch where we slept on our bunk beds had an outside door, locked, that I'm sure Grandma had never even suspected we knew how to open. Chuck had picked that lock with a bobby-pin of mine the first day we were at the cabin.

Suddenly Jenny whispered, "Look!" She was staring out into the grayness toward Wormwood, and all at once the twilight was gone completely and it was night.

"What?"

"See the light?"

We all saw it then. There wasn't any light at all in what we thought must be the livable wing of the ruins where the old lady who owned the place stayed, but there was certainly a light somewhere between the back of Wormwood and the lake—and it was moving! It wavered toward the lake and then back just a little. It came forward again—and went back. It looked as though somebody was hunting for something—or maybe beckoning someone—

The porch hammock where we were sitting was suddenly still, not swinging at all, but then I felt it quivering. Somebody was shivering, and it might have been me. It might have been all of us.

"Jenny?" I hardly dared breathe. It was silly—as if whatever held that light could hear us. "You know what a will-o'-wisp is?"

"Is it—a ghost?"

"Kind of. Not exactly. It's a mysterious light, like that one over there! Not the kind of light we have, not one you can turn on and off or even blow out like a candle. It's a supernatural one. It leads people to follow it—and then they fall in the lake and drown or get stuck in quicksand or walk over a cliff—"

"Then we won't follow it," Jenny said. "We'll go round it. Besides, there isn't any cliff. I don't know if there's quicksand or not. But we'll be sure not to go anywhere that light wants us to. We'll go the other way."

The child made sense. But I was still scared. I guess as you get older you do feel more cautious, until finally you're grown-up and don't dare to do anything at all any more.

I said, "I don't much want to go, tonight. Maybe we should explore it in the daytime first."

"Dare you," Jenny said softly. "Anyhow, Chuck and I are going. You don't have to."

I looked at that pale ghost-light out there in the dark, beckoning to us, and the wind shrieked something, but I couldn't tell what. And the light seemed to move closer.

"Gee Wiggles!" Chuck squealed. "I think it's coming after us!"

I wished like anything that I could take a dare, but I couldn't, being the oldest.

"Well, let's go to bed," I said. "Then when they're asleep—"

The Beckoning Light

Sarge snores, and Grandma breathes a certain way when she's asleep; Sarge says she's snoring too, but she says she's not. Anyhow, we could tell by their breathing when it was safe to get out of bed. They always leave the door open between their room and the sleeping porch so they can hear, Grandma says, if any of us needs them. The way they were sleeping, though, they couldn't have heard it if Russia had dropped the bomb. Jenny and I didn't have a bit of trouble climbing down from our top bunks and waking Chuck up without waking them. He had had to take a lower bunk because he's the youngest and we got our choice first. But sometimes I let him have a turn sleeping in my bunk when Grandma doesn't know. She's afraid he'll fall out. Nobody sleeps in the other lower bunk. I had suggested that Jenny's doll Annabelle and her Huckleberry Hound could sleep in it, but she likes them to sleep with her even if it's crowded. I can't convince her that she's too old for dolls. She says Annabelle isn't exactly a doll; she's a person. Huck, too. Now she stood on the frame of Chuck's bed and tucked them in before she would leave. She did have·better sense this time than to try to bring Annabelle along the way she usually does—she knew I wouldn't let her.

We had put on our pajamas so Grandma wouldn't suspect anything, but it didn't take long to change to shorts and shirts and sneakers. We had laid them ready where we could find them in the dark.

The door creaked a little when we opened it, but we managed to get out without waking the grandparents. We slipped around the front of the house, trying to be quiet, but I never heard anything as loud as the way twigs and acorns cracked under our feet. There were all sorts of queer night noises besides the wind in the trees—crickets chirping and July flies sawing away and frogs grumping and a whippoorwill ordering some other bird to do the whipping, I suppose—and something like somebody crying, way off somewhere in the dark.

"Listen!" Jenny said. "Hear that? Crying! I bet it's Jefferey's wife's ghost lost in that maze."

The prickles went up my back again, but I led the way down the path to where Sarge had anchored the boat at the foot of the hill. When I dared look across the lake, the strange light was still there, wavering nearer and then going back.

"I'm scared," Chuck whispered.

"Silly, it wouldn't be any fun if we weren't scared," Jenny told him.

"Is a will-o'-wisp any kin to a whippoorwill?" he asked after a while. He must have decided being scared was okay. We could talk now. We were far enough away from the cabin for them not to hear us, and we stopped a minute to rest and slap the mosquitoes.

"No, silly. A whippoorwill is a live bird," Jenny said positively. "A will-o'-wisp is a—a ghost of a light that maybe died. And now it wants us to die too. To drown in the lake. But we won't." She stared defiantly over at the frightening light.

"I bet it's just somebody with a flashlight looking for something," Chuck said, trying to believe it. He had brought along the flashlight he was so proud of, but I'd made him promise not to flash it unless I said okay. Jenny's pockets sagged with things she was carrying. She always brought everything she could think of, just in case we happened to need an aspirin box or a bottle of lightning bugs or a rusty nail or something useful like that.

"I bet it isn't." Jenny sounded pretty certain.

I was straining my eyes in the dark, to see the Becky-

Jen. Sarge had named the boat after us. The name was painted on her side. When Chuck wanted his name on her, too, Sarge told him boats were almost always named after girls. That satisfied Chuck; he's no sissy. Anyhow, they do call boats "she" in books. We always tried to remember, but sometimes we slipped up and called her "it."

"Jenny!" I whispered. "Can you see the boat? I can't."

"No—oo—" Jenny said.

"No," Chuck said. "I can't too. Can I turn on my flashlight, Beck?"

"No! Don't you dare." I was close enough now to see the water's edge, and there was absolutely nothing floating there, not even an empty old can. The Becky-Jen was gone.

"Be still!" Jenny whispered. "I hear something."

"I hear lots of things." Chuck was whispering too.

"Freeze!" I commanded. We all stood perfectly still behind a handy black-alder bush. It's one of the bylaws I wrote out for the Fine-Brain Club that when anybody—even Chuck—says "Freeze!" you have to.

Then we heard it clearly—somebody dipping a paddle in the water—and out of the dark the Becky-Jen slid up to the shore where Sarge anchors her. Somebody was in her.

Sarge wishes he could get rid of all the black alder on the place—he says it's not good for a thing, not even to turn red and look pretty in the fall. But it does make mighty fine cover. We stood there watching, and we were as good as invisible.

But we had to know who was in Sarge's boat. I reached over and took Chuck's flashlight out of his hand and flashed it on her, and there was that yellow-headed boy named Arie Chance. He had just jumped out of the boat, and was splashing, barefoot, toward the shore with the rope in his fist.

Well, a boy is nothing to be afraid of. "What are you doing with my grandpa's boat?" I said.

He was startled, of course. He stopped, and nearly

dropped the rope. He couldn't see us behind the brightness of the flashlight's beam, but I guess he could tell from my voice that I was a girl, so he wasn't scared either. He went ahead and tied the Becky-Jen up before he answered. Thinking up a story, I guessed.

"It was driftin' out in the lake," he said at last. "I come down here fishin' and seen it, so I waded out and caught the rope and brought it back."

I didn't know whether to say "Thank you" or "I don't believe a word of it." So I said, "Oh, you did?"

Chuck said, "Did you catch any fish?"

"Whole string of crappie." He reached back into the

boat and brought them out. It was more fish than all three of us together had ever caught.

"Gosh!" Chuck said respectfully. Then, "What are you gonna do with them?"

"Eat 'em, of course. Ma fries 'em in side-meat grease, and makes hush-puppies to go with 'em. Good eatin'. I catch this many near 'bout ever' night," he bragged.

"You mean you catch fish better at night than in the daytime?"

"Crappie you can. Sometimes I catch bass and bream in the daytime. I throw back the catfish and carp—they ain't much good to eat. Some folks do eat 'em, but—"

"You-all eat fish every day?" Jenny asked.

"In the summer we do. In the winter I trap rabbits for meat—and even right now I can catch a few. And I shoot squirrels in the fall, when I can get any shells for my gun."

"Gee Wiggles!" Chuck said, admiring him with his voice.

But Jenny said sternly, the way she does when she's laying down the law to Annabelle and Huck, "You stop that, you hear? Don't you dare kill any more of our rabbits and squirrels—you—you cannibal. They're our friends—"

"Reckon you buy all your meat at the store?"

I still had the flashlight trained on him, but I had turned it down out of his eyes by now, and he could see us. He looked us over, and we looked him over. He had no clothes on but faded swimming trunks. He was skinny—skinnier than Jenny, and that's really skinny—but he had more of a tan. In fact, he was so tanned that his yellow hair looked almost white. I guessed he was older than my boy-friend Mike back home, but he wasn't so very tall. He grinned at Jenny when she didn't answer, and said, "What's your name?"

"Jenny Dodd." She had to smile back. Then she remembered to say politely, "This is my sister Becky, and this is my brother Chuck. My real name is Jennifer. We already know yours. Grandma told us. It's Arie Chance!"

"Right. Well, what are you-all doin' out here, Jenny Dodd? Don't you kids know it's past your bedtime?"

"We're going ghost-hunting," she confided, and right there she broke one of the bylaws of the Fine-Brain Club. You aren't supposed to tell the secrets of the club to outsiders, not even if they torture you with hot irons. But maybe we hadn't actually said it was a Dead Secret, so it didn't count. "Look! Did you see that?" She pointed at the wavering light. "It's a will-o'-wisp, we think. And listen! Hear that crying? That's the ghost of Jefferey Winslow's wife wandering around in her white dress, lost in the maze. We're going to paddle the boat over there and try to see her."

He stared at the light, shaking his head. "Yep, I reckon it's queer enough, but I bet it ain't no ha'nt. As for somebody cryin', you're way off. That's nothin' but

31

a mournin' dove. Ain't you never heard a mournin' dove before? My granny used to say when you heard one it was a sign somebody was goin' to die, but Ma says not to take no stock in that. Shucks, birds can't tell when people are goin' to die."

"Gee Wiggles!" Chuck said again. "You know everything, don't you, Arie?"

"'Course not. I don't know hardly anything, my teacher says. I have to stay out of school a lot, to help Ma. I'm goin' to quit school when I'm sixteen and it's legal—that'll be a year from next December. I'll be old enough to get a real job then. They're puttin' up a new shoe factory over to Blairsville. I can make good money there."

"Wish I could quit school," Chuck said enviously. And he's only been in school a year.

"You do not," I told him. "You have to finish grammar school to get into high school to get into college and play football, remember? Arie, don't you want to go to college?"

"Naw. I want to get a job and make some money. Ma's been takin' care of us four kids by herself long enough."

I remembered about his father then and decided to change the subject. "Come on, you-all, if we're going we'd better hurry, before the storm starts. Look at the waves on the lake right now!" The heavy clouds were grumbling and the lightning flashed just about every minute. Wind ruffled the lake into waves that slapped the Becky-Jen's sides and rolled her.

"You kids can't go out on that lake," Arie said. "You'd be drowned. Why, I come back myself after I'd caught only about half enough, because it was gettin' so rough—" He stopped, and if it hadn't been dark I expect we could have seen him turn red. "I better tell you the truth," he said. "Ma says 'Tell the truth and shame the devil.' She says we got to tell the truth if we want to amount to anything. Well, I didn't exactly see your grandpap's boat driftin' out there. I got in the back end of it to sit and catch crappie. I do that sometimes—I don't see how he could mind. I don't hurt it a-tall, and one time I left him a mess of fish to kind of pay for the use of the boat."

"I remember!" Jenny said. "Sarge said he was mystified. He didn't see how those big-mouth bass could have jumped in the boat by themselves."

"And tonight somehow the boat got loose and started driftin' while I was in it. Good thing he left the paddle in it. Anyhow, you kids go on home and go to bed and forget it. You can't go out in a boat in any storm. And there's goin' to be a gully-washer in a minute."

I knew he was right, but there was something about a boy being so right that made me just plain contrary. "Who says we can't? It's our boat—it's got our names on it! We'll go out in it if we want to!"

Jenny said wistfully, "It's such a good night for

ghosts—and that's such a good place for them over there—and I don't suppose we'll ever find out about the will-o'-wisp if we don't go tonight while it's out haunting—"

Chuck said, being bossy as usual, "You girls better do what Arie says. He's the oldest." He was throwing my argument right back at me.

"He's not the oldest in the family. You two do what I tell you, not Arie."

"It's goin' to rain cats and dogs in a minute," Arie said. "Look, kids, I'm goin' to lay it right on the line now. If you go out in that boat, I got to wake your grandpap up and tell him on you. If I didn't and you got drowned, it'd be my fault. But if you won't go tonight, and go on back in the house before it rains, I'll take you over there tomorrow myself. I know a way to get in that old bunch of ruins without Old Lady Beadle seein' me from her side."

"A secret passage?" Jenny exclaimed, delighted.

"I don' know if you'd call it that. But it's secret all right, far's I know. 'Least nobody knows about it but me, I'm pretty sure. Well, is it a deal?"

"You can't see ghosts except at night," Jenny pointed out, pouting a little.

"But we could see better in the daylight if there are any footprints around where that light is," I said, "and maybe solve that particular mystery without actually tangling with a will-o'-wisp. And anyway, that's not a ghost crying, it's a mourning dove." I was about to give in and go back, not because of the secret passage—oh, no—but because I knew it really was dangerous to cross the lake at a time like this, and I do have pretty good sense sometimes.

"Well—you promise we'll go tomorrow?" Jenny begged.

"Scout's honor," I said. "Now we'll take a vote. All in favor of putting off the expedition to Wormwood until tomorrow say Aye."

They both said Aye, and I did too. Arie asked curiously, "What do you do that for?"

"We have a club. When you have a club, you have to take a vote when you want to decide anything," I told him.

Jenny whispered in my ear and I whispered in Chuck's, and we all said Aye again. Then Jenny asked Arie confidently, "You want to belong to the Fine-Brain Club?"

"What does it cost?"

"No dues."

"Well, all right." He looked at us doubtfully, and then grinned.

We gave him the grip and the password, which was "Bullet Louise" that day, and the secret call, which was the "bob-bobwhite" one. He could do it better than any of us—he sounded like a real bobwhite courting a lady bobwhite. Then we took a vote on meeting tomorrow at ten o'clock and got four Ayes, and started back to the cabin, bobwhiting as long as Arie could hear us and we could hear him. Lucky for us we had on our pajamas and were under our blankets before the thunder woke Grandma and she got up to lower the canvas curtains in the sleeping porch against the pouring rain. It was a howler, all right. A real gully-washer, as Arie said. We felt as if we were on a sailing vessel in a storm, with the canvas flapping.

I sure was glad Arie had given us such a good excuse not to be out on the lake right then. But I heard Jenny grumbling to herself—or to Annabelle, "That old boy. Spoiling everything—"

Well, he hadn't really. Even Jenny had to admit it next day when we four were actually inside the empty wing of old Jefferey's castle where the ghosts live, holding our breath and turning pale because we could hear something tapping on the other side of the wall. Tapping like a message from—the other world?

Secret Passage

We got up early the next morning and finished making our beds and helping with breakfast and the dishes and all. In fact we were so good that Grandma got suspicious. "What have you three been up to?" she asked me.

"Nothing," I said promptly. Rule Number One is to deny everything. Mama says it's a conditioned reflex, whatever that means.

Jenny said cagily, "Well, we were going to do something kind of dangerous last night, but we decided not to. So you owe us some bubble-gum for not doing it."

Grandma laughed, but she didn't give us the bubble-gum. "Just what was it you were going to do?"

"It was my idea. We wanted to go and hunt for

ghosts over yonder at that old castle-looking place," Jenny confessed.

"But you got cold feet?"

We nodded. Grandma went on, "No wonder. It does look like the setting for a horror movie or for the Addams family. But there aren't any real ghosts. Just a poor old lady who's had a lot of tragedy in her family and sees ghosts of her own there."

"Mr. Burdett told Jenny there were ghosts, the ghosts of Mr. Jefferey Winslow and his wife and a Confederate soldier who's buried in the garden—"

"People tell all sorts of stories about a place like that. Jenny mustn't believe everything she hears."

"But I like to believe in ghosts!" Jenny said earnestly. "Honest, Grandma. It makes shivers go up and down my back and I'm scared to go to sleep and it feels just wonderful!"

"Becky, you're old enough to have told Jenny No. You should have explained that there aren't really any ghosts—or have come to me and let me explain it. I can't have Jenny frightened."

"You don't understand, Grandma. She loves being scared to death. And I guess I do too, at least when I'm reading about ghosts."

Chuck signed in with us. "Me, too."

"Maybe I remember," Grandma said then. "Yes, I guess it's part of any happy childhood, to be able to feel 'zero at the bone,' as Emily Dickinson said, and yet enjoy it. But I'm glad you didn't go."

"Then can't we have some bubble-gum? And who's Emily—?" Jenny said. The dentist told her she couldn't chew gum any more after she got her braces, so she's trying to chew all the gum she can this summer before she has to go back for them in the fall.

"All right. One piece each. Emily Dickinson was a poet, one of the best American poets. Maybe the very best."

"I know her," I said. " 'There is no frigate like a book. . . .' " Grandma was pleased with me. I knew she would be. She likes to think I take after her because I read all the time. So then I asked, "Grandma, could we take a picnic lunch and go exploring today?" Rule Number Two is to tell them just enough so that they won't worry about us. "We'd be safe enough—we kind of met that boy Arie Chance, and he's going with us, and he's nearly fifteen, so he can keep Chuck from getting hurt. And he's really a pretty nice boy, Grandma."

"Well, I guess there's no harm in it, as long as there are three of you. The people around here say Mrs. Strickland is doing a good job of bringing up those children, in spite of—" She didn't finish what she was saying. She began to make bologna sandwiches and peanut-butter-and-jelly sandwiches for four. "I suppose you do need somebody to play with. And Arie is big enough to carry Chuck if he gets tired."

"Gee Wiggles! I don't want anybody to carry me!" Chuck said indignantly. "I'm no baby, Grandma. You forget, I grew up since last summer."

"So you did," Grandma said. She put in cookies too, and four bananas and four jaw-breakers. She wrapped up four dimes in a paper napkin and put them in the bottom of the lunch basket. "Don't lose them," she cautioned. "If you're over by the store at lunch time, you can buy yourselves each a soft drink. I guess you're going over to Mr. Burdett's old mill, aren't you? It's a pretty place for a picnic."

"Thanks, Grandma. We may end up over there," I said truthfully. "But we're going to do a lot of exploring before we stop to eat lunch." I slipped Chuck's flashlight into the basket when she wasn't looking.

"Well, be careful. Look where you're going so you won't step on a snake."

"We always do, Grandma," I said patiently. "You forget Jenny and I are girl scouts, and Chuck will be a cub next year. We've learned about the woods, at day-camp and all."

"Let's not get overconfident, now," Sarge said. "But I'm glad you-all are self-reliant. I think we can trust you to take care of yourselves and one another."

"Oh, you can!" Jenny assured him solemnly.

We took the lunch basket and said "Thanks,

Grandma" and kissed them both good-by. It's amazing how grandparents like to be kissed. You can take their minds off almost anything by kissing them. They didn't ask any more about where we were going. So of course they didn't tell us not to go. We know we have to obey our grandparents, but there's no law about going out of our way to give them things to tell us not to do.

Arie was waiting at the bend in the road. He had on faded blue jeans and a shirt that looked a little too big for him, like somebody older had worn it out and then given it to him. "Good you kids wore your jeans instead of shorts," he said approvingly. "This is goin' to be rough, if you really want to get inside that old place."

" 'Course we do. And you might give us credit for a little sense," Jenny told him. "We knew there'd probably be briars and things."

"Arie," I said, "tell us your plan of action."

He looked a little surprised—he probably didn't have any, really. But he said, "Well, you-all said you wanted to go over there to the old Winslow place, and of course Old Lady Beadle don't let nobody inside the gate. But we can go around the far side, where she can't see us, and climb over the wall. I found a dug-out tunnel that comes out by that little old tombstone, and the other end leads right into that empty wing. It ends up in a little space that seems to be in back of a fireplace. It's like bein' inside a closet only without any door—"

"It must have a secret door inside that you didn't

41

find," I said excitedly. "It must be a secret room where a Confederate could hide when the Yankees were coming. He'd have had to be a spy with valuable information for General Joe Wheeler, or else badly wounded—or he wouldn't have hidden; he'd have fought them off singlehanded. The ghost was a Confederate hero, wasn't he? See, he must have been escaping by the secret tunnel, because they say he was buried where he fell. The Federal scouts must have seen him just as he came out, and shot him."

"Were they all heroes?" Chuck asked. "All of our side?"

" 'Course they were," Jenny assured him.

I asked, "How did you know about the tunnel, Arie?"

"I go all over that place, huntin' rabbits. She ain't never caught me yet. I even set traps—she don't see 'em. She's old, you know—she don't get about much. One day when I was settin' a trap I stumbled into the hole at the end of the tunnel. It sort of caved in. I thought it was a rabbit hole and went to diggin' after him, and pretty soon I found out it was a regular tunnel that somebody had dug. It's got supports, and beams across the top. It was full of cobwebs and roots and all, but I cleared it out and then put stuff over the hole to hide it. We got to crawl, but we can get through all right."

"Weren't you scared?" Jenny said in awe. "Mr. Burdett says Mrs. Beadle lives in one side, and the other wing is where the ghosts live. They do just come out at night, I guess. But weren't you scared at all?"

"Naw. I never did find the door from the tunnel into the room, if there is any door. Besides, I ain't scared of ha'nts. Ma says they won't bother you if they got nothin' against you, and I never done nothin' to any of 'em. Well, come on, if you want to go."

"We'll find the secret door!" Jenny said happily. "We'll get in that room and see if ghosts live there. There ought to be some signs of them if they do."

"I don't exactly think we ought to trespass," I said. "It's trespassing if you go into somebody's house when they didn't invite you."

"It don't say No Trespassin'," Arie said. "And it ain't really her house, where she lives. I wouldn't go into her house. Ma'd tan my hide. But this is just a empty old house where nobody lives, kind of next door to her house."

"Nobody 'cept ghosts," Jenny insisted hopefully.

"We won't bother nothin'," Arie argued. "It's all right to go on anybody's place and hunt, Ma says, if there ain't a sign sayin' No Trespassin'."

"Well, all right," I agreed. He made it sound okay. "But we mustn't break in. If we can't find a way in without breaking in, we'll have to come back without going inside. All in favor say Aye."

They all said Aye, and we hiked around the edge of the lake, with Arie leading the way, and we got beggar-lice all over our jeans. When we were nearly in front of Wormwood, with only a lot of trees and stuff between, he turned back to us and said, "Oh—about that light you kids got so het up about last night—"

"The will-o'-wisp?" Jenny said breathlessly.

"I come over here early this mornin' to see if I could find out what it was. There warn't any footprints in the mud a-tall." We found out later why he didn't want us to do our own investigating of that strange light, but at the time his doing it for us seemed reasonable.

"That's funny," I said. "Do you think it actually could have been a will-o'-wisp, Arie?"

"Well, it wasn't nobody with a flashlight, or they'd have left tracks."

"It rained," Chuck reminded him. "Tracks might've washed away."

"Good thinking, boy," I told him.

But Jenny chose not to hear him. "Anybody human would've left tracks," she whispered fearfully. "So it wasn't—human—"

"Ha'nts don't generally carry lights," Arie said.

"They carry all kinds of things," I told him. "The ghost of Anne Boleyn carries her own head."

"Who's she?"

"A queen who got beheaded a long time ago and can't rest quiet in her grave with her head off. Oh, let's don't bother with English history now," I said. "It must be a will-o'-wisp—if there are any such things as will-o'-wisps."

"I think there are," Jenny said positively.

"Let's take a vote," Chuck said.

"I don't think you can vote on things like that," I said. "Besides, it's daytime and will-o'-wisps are never seen except at night. Let's table the motion instead and get on with the secret tunnel. All in favor say Aye." We all did.

Then Chuck said, "All in favor of eating lunch now say Aye."

We all voted No, except Chuck. "It's only about ten-thirty, prob'ly," Jenny told him, squinting at the sun. "We have to wait till the sun is right straight up overhead before we eat."

"Gee Wiggles!" Chuck said, looking at his wrist where his Roy Rogers watch used to be before he broke it winding it too tight. "My stomach must be fast."

We followed Arie around the old crumbling wall single file, bending low so our heads wouldn't show over the top of it. The stones were green with moss, and Jenny saw a green lizard run along the top. Chuck wanted to catch it for a pet, but we voted No.

It seemed a long way around to the spot where Arie was taking us, but he said some trees grew over the wall there and Mrs. Beadle wouldn't see us climb it. When we got to his climbing place, we saw what he meant. The Ghost Wing and the ruins of the castle itself and some of the old weed-grown garden were between us and Mrs. Beadle's wing, and there were plenty of trees for a screen.

The wall was almost falling down. It wasn't hard to get over it, though we had to be careful not to slide down when the rocks gave way under our feet. You could sprain an ankle that way. Arie gave us each a hand, in turn; so Chuck didn't mind being helped over. We hung the lunch basket on a limb just outside the wall, safe from ants and well hidden by leaves.

"Where's the confederate spy's grave?" Jenny asked. "Where the ghost comes out bleeding?"

"That little old tombstone? Over there." Arie pointed, and we all saw the small gray headstone under a big oak tree that was probably little when the soldier was buried there. We tiptoed toward it. There was a kind of solemn hush in that old tangled-up garden. The sun was hazy and the trees were still and the light was gray-green under the twisted branches. We tried to read the letters cut on the headstone, but they were filled in with mold, and lichens made them the same color as the stone.

"I see the hole!" Chuck said. It went right into the side of the low hill. Arie had hidden it pretty well with branches and rocks, but Chuck can always find things.

After he found the Christmas presents a couple of times, Santa Claus had to give up.

Arie went first, using Chuck's flashlight because he didn't have one of his own, and he told me to be last because I was next oldest. We had to crawl on our hands and knees, and it was dirty and scary and we could hardly breathe. I couldn't help wondering about snakes and moles and rats. Then I thought, What if the whole thing caved in on us? Grandma and Sarge would never know what had become of us.

"Well, at least we'd be already buried if it caved in," Jenny said as if she could read my mind, the gruesome child. "They wouldn't need to have any funeral." Her voice sounded muffled and yet it echoed hollowly, like a ghost's.

"Shut up," I said. I could hear Chuck scrambling along just ahead of me, breathing hard.

"Sssh-shh," Arie said. "This is the end of it. Now, when I push this thing out of the way we'll be behind the old chimney and we can stand up." He shoved at the dead end of the tunnel and it swung open like a cathole. We pushed our way through.

There was hardly room for the four of us to stand, even close together. The flashlight showed us the old bricks of the wall, with cobwebs hanging everywhere, and the wide dusty boards of the floor.

"Gee Wiggles!" Chuck whispered. "Looka there.

What's that?" He pointed to the corner. There was an old dirty crockery thing that looked like a cup, only much too big.

Arie said, "Don't you know what that is? You never seen a thunder mug before?"

"No. What's a thunder mug?"

"I reckon your Grandma and Grandpap must have plumbin' in their place." The way he said it made it sound like having a regular bathroom was a crime or something.

"Sure they have, but—"

"Shut up, Chuck," I said. "I'll explain it to you later." I didn't know too much about the pioneers' bathrooms, myself, but I did know what a chamber pot was for. Originally, that is. Diane's mother got one from an antique shop and uses it to put flowers in, for goodness' sake.

"Let's find the secret door," Jenny said impatiently. "I want to get in there and explore the ghost's house."

"In books people always go around tapping on the walls until they find a place that sounds hollow," I said. "But we're inside the place that would sound hollow. If we were on the other side, now—"

"One thing sure, they didn't get in through the fireplace," Arie said. He flashed the light on the bricks, and they looked awfully solid, for such old bricks.

"I remember now!" I told them. "This is what they

used to call a priest's hole. A long time ago in England, when they changed religions, Cromwell's soldiers were trying to kill all the priests, and good Catholics hid them to save their lives."

"But this was for hiding wounded Confederate soldiers or spies from the Yankees," Jenny reminded me.

"Yes, I read about that too. Lots of the old plantation houses had secret places like this."

"I'm getting too hot," Chuck said. "Let's try to get out of here. How are we gonna get out, Beck?"

"Well, if there's no crack in the bricks, the door couldn't be there. And the walls are bricked in. The only other place is the floor." I took out my girl scout knife, and with Arie holding the light, I tried to pry up the boards by putting the knife end into the cracks.

"There!" Jenny said, so excited she could hardly speak. "Poke it there. It looks like it would come open —see—" Sure enough, there were almost invisible hinges. A section of the floor—on the opposite side from the tunnel where we had come in—was a trap door. Arie took the knife and pried. It resisted, but after a while he must have accidentally touched the secret spring. The board came up so suddenly that he would have fallen backward if I hadn't been squatting behind him with Jenny packed in behind me. There was a space barely big enough for a man to crawl through on his stomach, and he couldn't be a very fat man, either. But all the Confederates were thin, because they didn't have enough to eat. The space led off in the other direction from the tunnel, down under the floor.

"You dare see where it goes?" I asked Arie.

"Sure I dare." He let himself down into it through the trap door, the light flashing ahead of him. His voice came back to us, smothered under the floor. "It's only a little place, a sorta dip in here under the boards. It's got another openin' to get out at." Kneeling around the edge of the trap door in the priest's hole, we could see him lying flat on one ear, prying with the knife at the possible opening. "Got it!" He pulled himself upward by his hands. "Come on through," he called back softly. "One at a time. Becky last. The hole comes out into a sorta closet."

Jenny and Chuck scrambled through, but I saw something tucked away on a little dusty ledge formed by the crosspieces under the floor and the supports holding them up. "Wait a minute!" I reached for it. It was a small leather-covered book. The leather was half eaten away and some of the pages were tattered on the edges.

I could hear my heart beating as I slipped the book into my jeans pocket and climbed out of the hole. That book—I was sure it had been hidden there by the Confederate soldier who was shot as he came out into the garden. His dead hands were the last hands that had touched it—until I touched it. It made me shiver to think of it—but I was thrilled deep down into my stomach. I couldn't help wondering what he had written that he had to hide there, when his life was in danger.

The closet opened into an empty room, dusty and cobwebby. Our feet made the only prints in the thick gray coating on the floor. If there were ghosts living there, they hadn't left any footprints. The ceiling was high, and strips of old moldy wallpaper hung down from it. A vine had crawled in like a green snake where a board was loose between the wall and the floor.

"What's the matter?" Arie said. "Why'd you say 'Wait a minute'?"

"I found something," I panted. "A book. It might be—"

"Oh, just a book," Arie said.

"What do you mean, 'just a book'?" I said hotly. "Haven't you got any imagination at all? Why, it's a kind of notebook that poor Confederate spy hid there when he was escaping from the Yankees—only he didn't escape—so it must have been something he didn't want them to see. I can hardly wait to read it—" and I started to take it out of my pocket.

Only I didn't.

It was just then that we heard the tapping on the other side of the wall.

Lost in the Maze

"The ghost!" Jenny said.

Well, that was all it took to start a panic. There are times when a person can be brave—maybe—but not when the other three, including the oldest, who's a boy, are breaking and running for the closest window. I ran too.

The window glass was already out—we didn't have to break it. We scrambled through it so fast the glass would've broken, though, if there'd been any. Breathing hard, I grabbed Chuck's hand and followed Arie and Jenny, who had already disappeared behind some tall bushes in the weedy overgrown garden. We stumbled through a corridor of black-green shade, where branches twined into a roof that shut out the sun overhead. Brambles caught at our feet. The gloomy, leafy lane twisted and turned. In places we could hardly get through it, and after a while I began to feel as though we were going around in circles. "Look," I said. "You-all wait a minute. You know what? I think we've found the maze."

"Where?" Arie asked. "What do you mean?"

"Right here. We're in it. And we probably can't find our way out again."

"We're lost?" Jenny said. "No! We may not have a compass, but we can look for the moss on the north side of the trees and—" She looked at the trunks of the ancient bushes that had grown into trees towering over our heads, and then added accusingly, "But these things have moss on all their sides—"

"We can just go back the same way we came, can't we, if we want to?" Arie said. He sounded as though he didn't much want to, though.

"You sure we can?"

He turned and started back, to show us. We didn't follow him, because we could glimpse him through the branches, wandering and turning, and then butting his way back into a path that—you guessed it—brought him right back to where we were standing. He said slowly, "I reckon I see what you mean, Becky. I've never been way in here before. It's sort of like bein' in a rabbit trap."

"That's the way it is in a maze," I told him. "We could wander around in here for days and nights—"

53

Jenny said, "This is where she comes, crying, at night?"

"How d'you know?" Arie said to me. "How do you know it's one of them whatchamacallits?"

"I've read about them. They were popular in gardens in Queen Elizabeth's time. The first Queen Elizabeth."

"Readin's no good. It won't get us out of here."

I didn't really feel so very superior just because I knew the name of the trap we were in, but I told him, "Reading always comes in useful sometime. You don't know when you might need something you read—or even studied in school." Just then, as if to prove even to myself that what I was saying was true, the story of Theseus and the labyrinth popped into my head, straight out of *Myths Every Child Should Know*. "For instance," I told Arie, "when Theseus went into the labyrinth after the Minotaur, he unwound some thread so he could find his way back out again. And didn't Tom Sawyer do the same thing when he and Becky Thatcher were in the cave with Injun Joe? Those are people in books. Now if we had a thread—"

Jenny reached into her bulging pocket. "Here." She produced a ball of fishing cord. "Thought it might come in handy," she explained matter-of-factly.

"You don't happen to have an apple in there, do you?" Chuck asked.

"No. You hungry? Here's an old beat-up cough drop you can have if you want it."

Chuck actually took it.

Arie ignored them as well as the fishing cord, "I get the idea," he said. "But we don't need the fishin' cord. It would be plumb foolish to use stuff like that just because you read it in a book. See, we can just break the branches a certain way as we go, and see our own trail. I don't know why I didn't think of that. We'd prob'ly be able to find our way back the same way we came just by lookin' for the branches we already broke gettin' through."

"You're right," I said. It was good thinking, for a boy. "Theseus and Tom were both in caves. They didn't have any broken twigs to follow. And that's why the Indians were so careful never to break a twig, so the scouts couldn't follow their trail. So we can do it backwards and follow our own."

"But we don't want to go back there," Jenny pointed out. "Weren't we trying to get away from the ghosts? It scared me so I forgot about wanting to see one."

"I don't even believe it was a ghost," I said. "Suppose the tapping was just a tree branch hitting against a windowpane?"

"S'pose it wasn't?" Jenny said. "Why'd you run if it was? Besides, there weren't any windowpanes. They were all broken out."

"You know what I mean. And I ran because we had to keep together, and you-all were running. But I don't think we should have run." I wasn't too scared at this point, because it was nearly noon and ghosts just don't show at noon, unless they are mighty mixed-up ghosts. And it was hard to believe we could really be very far from the edge of that silly maze. It couldn't be all that big, I reasoned. "Anyhow," I said, doing some of what Daddy calls "tangent" thinking, "we don't have to go back. We can start from here, leaving a trail of broken twigs so we'll know if we're going in circles. If we strike out at a right angle from the path, maybe we can work our way across the maze."

"It's time to eat lunch," Chuck said. "I know it is. I wish we'd brought it with us."

"I don't," Jenny said. "If we had, we'd have sure lost it back there when we heard the ghost tapping! He could be eating our peanut-butter-and-jelly sandwiches right now. Give me back my fishing cord, if you aren't going to use it," she asked me. "It's my special lucky drop line that I caught my big fish on that time."

I gave it back. "Thanks anyway, Jen. It would've come in handy if we'd been in a cave." She stuck it in her shirt front. She looked like a skinny boa constrictor that had swallowed a big frog.

"Well, let's try it," Arie said. I noticed that he looked at me with a bit more respect now, as if to admit that I did have a good idea occasionally, even if I read books.

We struck out through the bushes, and of course they had been planted terribly close together, on purpose, so as to make them impossible to get through. Whoever laid it out—old Jefferey or his wife—must have wanted their maze to have solid walls, green ones. And now it had grown so much more than it was even meant to that it was like thrusting at a boxwood barrier in a nightmare. And not only the original boxwood, which they'd meant to keep nice and smooth and trimmed, but all kinds of other stuff had grown up in between. Most of it had thorns. Ironwood and blackberry vines.

After a while Jenny panted, "I'm tired. That old ghost's not chasing us any more. Let's stop and rest. All in favor—"

We were all in favor. Jenny and I leaned against each other, sitting on the ground back to back like those peon bookends Daddy brought us from Mexico. Chuck lay on his stomach and started pestering an ant with a twig, making it climb over and then putting a bigger twig in front of it just when it thought it was getting away. "He's in an ant maze," he explained when Jenny started helping him. "He'll prob'ly never find his way home. You leave him alone. Get yourself an ant of your own if you want to poke one."

Arie just sat against a tree with his head leaning on his knees. I couldn't tell what he was thinking, but I guessed he was more than likely wishing he had never seen the Dodds.

Then I remembered the little old book in my jeans pocket. "Say, let's just take a quick look and see what this is, while we're resting."

Arie wasn't much interested, but Jenny reached for it. "Look out, it's crumbly," I told her. "Don't touch it. I'll tell you what it says. I'll let you hold it later."

Jenny pouted, but she didn't bother me while I tried to make out the dim brown handwriting on the yellowish pages.

"I think it's a diary," I said excitedly. "And it belonged to a Winslow all right—there's his name in the front. Not Jefferey—this one was Colonel Richard Brevard Winslow." Silverfish had eaten a bit of his name, but I could make it out.

"I bet he was Mrs. Beadle's grandfather," Jenny said. "Mr. Burdett said it was her grandfather who was buried in the garden—the Confederate soldier. And her name was Winslow before she married Mr. Beadle, Mr. Burdett said."

"Then it was all before she was born." I was figuring out loud. "How old did he say she is?"

"Eighty-five."

"Then she was born in 1881—sixteen years after the War ended. So if her father were at least twenty years older than she was, and if his father were at least twenty years older again, then Colonel Winslow might have been just in his twenties when he got killed—" I was trying to see him in my mind. He would have been tall and handsome in his gray uniform, a dashing soldier like Jeb Stuart . . . "They got married young, in those days."

"How do you know all that stuff?" Arie asked me. "About that old War and all?"

"We studied the War Between the States in history last term," I explained. "It was interesting, because our own great-greatgrandfather was with Fighting Joe Wheeler, in the Fifth Georgia Cavalry. He rode his horse Dixie all through the War, and his best friend was shot off a horse right beside him, but our great-great-grandpa never got a scratch, and neither did Dixie. That good old horse brought him all the way home after the War and then dropped dead. Mama says they used to have Great-great-grandpa's sword around the house when she was a little girl, but she doesn't know what ever became of it. But hush up now; I want to see what's in this diary."

"I wasn't the one doin' all the talkin' about great-great-grandpaps," Arie said. I guessed he was just feeling out of it. Probably his great-great-grandpa was one of those mountaineers who hid out in the hills and wouldn't fight on either side.

I was reading as fast as I could, but the handwriting was very faded, and it wasn't easy. It wasn't really a diary—I mean he hadn't kept it from day to day all through the War. It seemed to be a record of what he was doing just for a short time at the end of the War. It skipped some days, but each time he wrote in it, he put the date. And after I had read a little bit, I saw why he had thought it was necessary to write it down. It was very important.

"What does it say?" Jenny was just as impatient as I was. Daddy says she has intellectual curiosity too, though she doesn't do quite as much regular thinking as I do. Arie pretended to be bored. He leaned back and shut his eyes and acted like he was asleep. Chuck went on playing with his ant. I skimmed through the pages, getting more and more excited.

"Wait till you hear! Why, it looks like Colonel Winslow wasn't a spy after all. He must have been one of the officers in charge of guarding all the money and bars of gold and silver the Confederacy had left over when the War was about to end! You remember in history, about the lost Confederate gold, Jenny? They brought it to Georgia—"

"Let me see," Jenny insisted. She was on her knees looking over my shoulder. The first page, dated April 2, 1865, read: "Mr. Davis got General Lee's telegram in church this morning while the hymn was being sung. I was sitting several pews behind him and his party. When I saw the President get up quietly and walk out after looking at the piece of paper, I left too, of course, and so did Bob. The President told us General Lee said he could not possibly save Richmond, and that we would have to go South immediately. He spent the afternoon securing the Treasury's gold and silver money and bullion, and getting his official papers packed. Bob and I, with a few other officers and Cabinet members, helped pack the money—half a million dollars, more or less, all that was left in the Treasury—into money belts, shot bags, and three cast-iron chests. It was turned over to Captain Parker, who was detailed by Secretary Mallory to take charge of the money train, with about two hundred men to guard it. We left on the President's special train tonight, and the money train came right behind us. Two thousand cavalrymen rode after us. The troops will probably evacuate Richmond. I hope we get to Georgia."

Then there was an entry dated April 4, 1865, at Danville, Virginia: "Today the President called us all together and divided the government expense money, some $35,000 in gold, among us for safe keeping while we are traveling. If some of us are captured, others may escape with funds to go on with. I have stowed the gold coins in a money belt which I wear, and in two shot bags which I carry. They are heavy, but I dare not lay them aside. When we transfer to the wagon trains I may put them in the saddlebags as I ride. We are to separate into two groups, the better to avoid capture, but Bob and I will remain with the President."

"What does it all mean, Beck?" Jenny asked.

I was so excited I had even forgotten that we were lost in the maze at Wormwood. "The President he's talking about was Jefferson Davis, of course, the President of the Confederacy. And the gold—you remember, Jenny, you studied it too, didn't you, in Georgia history in the fifth grade? The lost Confederate gold! It's one of the most mysterious chapters in history, Miss Wayne said, what happened to it all. Some of it was found, of course, but not nearly all. Well, it looks like Colonel Winslow was one of the officers who helped bring it to Georgia. After Lee surrendered at Appomattox. Let's see what else is in here."

I deciphered his handwriting as well as I could, and figured out that Colonel Winslow had stayed with the fugitive President while he dodged around for about a month, with the Federal troops right behind them. Probably he was one of Davis's military aides, and of course the Yankees were trying to capture all the Confederate officers and leaders even after the surrender. The money was transferred, he said, to wagons and back to railroad cars and back again to wagons. Sometimes Mrs. Davis and the children were with the money wagons, but not always. Colonel Winslow was helping her part of the time, but mostly he stayed with the President. They got separated from the money wagons for a time but after a while Captain Parker caught up with President Davis and delivered the Confederate Treasury to him. That seems to have happened at Abbeville, South Carolina, according to the entry in the notebook for May 2, 1865: "General Duke ordered the chests and boxes transferred to our wagon train this morning, and detailed several troops of cavalry to guard it, and we started again for Washington, Georgia. Nearer home every day! The President asked that a rider be sent ahead to make sure there were no Yanks in town. Bob volunteered, and is now gone, while we camp on the bank of the river."

The next note was dated May 4, 1865: "Bob came back last night to report that the coast is clear—no organized Yanks closer than General Upton's troops, near Augusta, as far as he can learn. But there are scouts out everywhere, looking for us. One of them took a long shot at Bob, but missed. We crossed the Savannah River this morning into Wilkes County. The President ordered General Breckinridge to pay the soldiers with silver specie, right there—the last payroll of the Confederacy, I suppose it may be. Each man got about thirty-two dollars. The rest of the money and the bullion were carried into Washington-Wilkes and delivered to Mr. Clark. I understand he has stored it for the night in a vault under Mr. Shelverton's store, guarded by men he can trust."

He described in the next entry, May 5, how Mr. Davis held the last meeting of his Cabinet there in Washington-Wilkes and dissolved the Confederacy, and how he had to take off again because General Upton was about to catch them. "The President told us to leave him now and save ourselves in any way we can, since the Yankees are trying to capture us all, now that the War is over, to try us as traitors. But, he said, it may not be safe to go to our homes; they will look for us there. General Toombs barely escaped by the back door of his home while his wife talked to the Yanks at the front. He is going to Europe if he can get away. Bob wants to go with him. I told the President there is a hiding place at Winwood if I can get there, and I tried to persuade him to come with me, but he has to get to Mrs. Davis; he feels he must be with her. He left the gold we have been carrying personally in the keeping of myself and the others, to be used for helping returning Confederate soldiers and their families—all of whom I fear will sadly need help. Some, fearing capture, are burying the gold here until times are more settled. But I will carry what I hold to Winwood, if I can, before hiding it."

"He brought it here?" Jenny said. "Gold?"

"Like pirate treasure?" Chuck asked, letting the ant go at last and sitting up. "Did he bury it? Can we dig for it?"

"Wait a minute! He says on the next page that he did get it to Winwood. Let's see if he—yes, he did."

"Did what?"

"He wrote this last page while he was hiding in the priest's hole. He must have had a candle or something. Of course the family gave him what he needed in there—"

"Tell us what he said! Who cares about the family?"

"He put the gold coins in a metal box and buried it 'under the rock on the creek where Eleanor and I used to play.' He says 'nobody will ever find it there, but if anything happens to me, Eleanor will know how to find it, because it is under the Indian stone.' Then he says he is tired of staying hidden and is going to 'slip out tonight and reconnoiter.' So that was when they shot him. Poor Colonel Winslow."

"Eleanor must have been his little sister," Jenny said.

When I realized what that last page meant, I got so excited I could hardly talk. "You see? This means he hid the book and crawled out and was killed, and nobody ever found the book, so nobody knew at all about the gold! Not Eleanor or anybody."

"So maybe it's still there?"

"Maybe. If only we could find the creek—and then the Indian rock! But that could mean anything. It could be a rock that looks like an Indian's head or his profile, or a rock with Indian marks on it, or just any old rock where they built a campfire when they played Indians—"

"Well, we could find the creek and then we might see a rock that looked like an Indian one, somehow," Jenny said. "It's worth a try, isn't it, Beck?"

"It sure is!"

"But would it belong to us?" Jenny asked worriedly.

Chuck contributed, "Finders keepers."

I said, "I don't know. But I think there's a law that

if the real owners don't claim something that's found, the person who finds it gets it after a certain time. Nobody could possibly know who owns the Confederate gold after all this time. Besides, he said it was to be used for Confederate soldiers and their families, and we're some of a Confederate soldier's family. So maybe—"

Arie came to life then and said, "You kids mean you're goin' to dig around for money hereabouts?"

"All in favor of digging for gold say Aye!" There were only three Ayes.

"Count me out," Arie said. "And you better not."

"Why, Arie!" Jenny said. "Don't you want to find it? We'd divide it four ways, and your mama wouldn't have to sell whatever it is she sells any more."

"What do you mean by that? She sells yarbs, that's all."

"What are yarbs?" Chuck asked. I thought Arie meant herbs, and I was right.

"Roots and leaves and bark and stuff that're good for medicine. Ginseng root is the best to sell, but people pay good money for sassafras too, and wild-cherry bark and yellowroot and heartleaf root and devil's shoestring and mullein leaves and lots of others. Ma gathers 'em in the woods and washes 'em nice and dries 'em, and lots of folks buy 'em."

"Well, anyway, if you brought her some gold coins she wouldn't have to work so hard, and you wouldn't have to quit school and work in the shoe factory."

"I ain't goin' to help you kids if you go snoopin' around diggin' for money."

"Why not? Even if we didn't find it, it'd be fun to look."

Arie only looked stubborn and shook his head. "I just ain't, that's all."

"Then you can't belong to the Fine-Brain Club any more."

"All right, so I don't belong. Now let's try again to get out of here."

I had been thinking while Jenny argued with Arie, and it did seem odd that he wouldn't want to dig for the gold. But I was uncomfortable mostly, I guess, because I knew we didn't really have any right to dig for it either. Arie had started to break through the maze again, but I said, "Wait a minute. I guess we've got to try to find the way back the same way we came, by the branches we broke getting this far."

"What now?" Arie said, looking as if he'd like for me to vanish.

"And meet a ghost?" Jenny squeaked, not sure whether she still wanted to or not.

"No. Not exactly. We've got to go and find old Mrs. Beadle, that's all. It's the only right thing to do. We can't take this book. It's not ours. We don't steal things. We've got to go and give it to her, no matter how scared we are. It was her grandfather's, so now it be-

longs to her, just as our great-great-grandfather's sword
would belong to us if we ever found it. And besides,
after reading what he was thinking that day, I almost
feel as if I know Colonel Winslow, and I like him, and
we can't steal his book. Don't you see?"

"And the gold is hers, too?"

"I don't know. There's something in the rules about
the person whose land buried treasure is found on getting some part of it. And anyway, she could say it was
Colonel Winslow's if she wanted to claim it. But I
don't mind; maybe she needs it worse than we do. Or
the government might confiscate it, because after all the
United States won the War. But that would be all
right, too. I'd like to hunt for it anyhow. It would be
lovely fun to find out what became of some of the lost
Confederate gold. Miss Wayne would probably give me
an A in history. The only thing is, we can't go away
from here with this little book."

"Could we just leave it here?"

"We could," I said slowly, half tempted to. "But
that would be kind of mean, wouldn't it? She'd probably never find it, and the rain would ruin it. After all,
she'd want it if she knew anything about it, just because it was her grandpa's. And it's too valuable a thing
historically to be left without telling anybody. The diary
itself is probably worth a lot of money to people who
collect old Civil War records and stuff like that. And

it's hers. So I'm going back and give it to her. You-all don't have to come if you don't want to, but I kind of wish you would."

"I'll go with you," Jenny said, looking scared but determined.

"Me too," Chuck said, slipping his hand into mine. It was a nice vote of confidence, but I could tell he was thinking, too, that the lunch was over in that direction. "Daddy told me to look after you."

"I don't want to get mixed up with Old Lady Beadle," Arie said. "And I ought to get back home anyhow. Ma'll have dinner on the table."

"Grandma packed enough lunch for all four of us," I told him.

"I'll eat his," Chuck offered.

"You aren't scared of Mrs. Beadle, are you, Arie?" Jenny challenged.

"Naw, I ain't scared. I just don't want to. I ain't goin' to help you dig for any money, either, and I don't think you ought to do it. I think you-all ought to mind your own business. That's what I think."

Arie had changed. All of a sudden he didn't seem to want to be nice to us any more. He looked like he was mad at all of us, and mad at the whole world besides. I felt a little bit sorry for him, because he probably didn't want to feel that way. But why had he changed so quickly?

"I don't know what we did to make you mad," I said,

"but I'm sorry. You go ahead and get out of the maze the quickest way, and go on home, if you want to. But we're going back to give Mrs. Beadle her book, and then maybe she'll give us permission to hunt for the gold for her."

"You're gon' to dig for it, then?"

"I don't know. That depends. But Arie, you can at least tell us where the creek nearest to Wormwood is. You must know all the creeks around here."

He said slowly, "There ain't no creeks around here." He didn't look me in the eyes, and I knew he was telling a big, fat lie.

The Long-lost Diary

I wondered if Arie had already come across the gold while he was poking around setting rabbit traps, and didn't want anybody trying to find out what had become of it. But no, their family wouldn't have been so poor if he had. They could have bought meat at the grocery store. It was a real puzzler, why he was acting this odd way.

He had started again to break through the maze at right angles to the path, to get out. "Well, goodby, Arie," Jenny said to his back. "See you later, alligator."

We started to backtrack, single file, the other way, to find the original path. I was in front, Chuck in the middle. It wasn't too hard to pick up our trail; the main trouble was that it was still rough going. We looked like real tramps by the time we got to the end. Our jeans and shirts were torn and full of beggar-lice—and those horrid little seeds cling so you can't ever get them all off. There were bloody scratches on our ankles and hands and even on Jenny's and Chuck's faces, and I found out later that I had some on mine, too. But at least we felt right. We didn't have scratches on our consciences. We wouldn't have changed places with Arie even if he was already home eating his dinner. Besides, the whole thing still felt like an adventure—the best one the Fine-Brain Club had ever had.

We came out at last where the sun was, and stood looking at the ruins of Wormwood. We hadn't had time really to look at them, before. I felt shaky, just because it was all so strange.

There was the Ghost Wing, with the broken window we had tumbled out of so fast. The other windows were just holes without panes. Then there was the castle. It looked as if a strong wind could blow it down—just shell walls of old brick with the edges of the towers broken, a skeleton of a staircase, and a half-fallen-down brick chimney with the fireplace still looking almost like a fireplace under it, and all through the rooms, trees growing up through rotted floors, and blooming honeysuckle vines tangling in the doorways. The smell of the honeysuckle was like the lady ghost's perfume after she walked here. It all looked so abandoned, so absolutely, utterly desolate. I felt the same way Jenny did when she whispered, "I'm so sorry for old Jefferey, Beck. He wanted it to be so grand for his wife, and then she had to go and die. And now look at it, and nobody cares—"

"Maybe Mrs. Beadle does. And we do."

Chuck picked honeysuckle blooms and sucked the ends for the honey. "Want some?" he said. Jenny and I weren't *that* hungry.

The wing on the other side of the ruins, the place where Mrs. Beadle lived, looked just like any other house that was all run down, but you could see how both it and the Ghost Wing had been meant to join up to the castle. If it had been finished, it would have spread out like two *L*'s back-to-back, the towers and all in the middle. It faced toward the road, with the back of the castle toward the lake, and down there behind it we could see a few tumble-down outbuildings and what looked like a one-room servant house (or slave cabin?) that still seemed pretty good, for its age.

"Well?" Jenny said. "What do we do now?" She looked scared, and serious.

"Whatever we do, let's eat first," Chuck said.

"No. Let's go on and get it over with, and then we can enjoy our picnic. All in favor say Aye." Jenny and I outvoted Chuck.

Well, we didn't go very fast, but we did go. We walked right up to the front steps, pausing once in a while to let out the breaths we were sort of holding. Chuck nearly fell through the broken step. I caught him and lifted him across it, and all three of us stood in a row, trying to get up nerve enough to knock at the big old door where the paint was peeling off. All of a sudden the sun went under a cloud and everything got dark and gray and I wondered just for a minute if Mrs. Beadle really could be a witch.

"Go on and knock," Jenny whispered. "You're the oldest."

I had to. But before I could make my knuckles move to the wood, the door suddenly opened.

We jumped back and nearly fell down the steps. It was dark inside, and at first we couldn't see anybody. But a voice said, "You children come on in here." It was so old and wispy a voice that it seemed like the way cobwebs would sound if they could make a noise.

We couldn't give back the book if we didn't go in; so we had to. After all, Mrs. Beadle was a real person, not a ghost. She couldn't hurt us. I was thinking we could even outrun her, if necessary. I took Chuck by the hand and told myself, "Just put one foot after the other, that's the way. Now." When I looked up from my feet, Jenny was holding out her hand politely to the oldest old lady I've ever seen, and saying, "How do you do? I'm Jenny Dodd, and this is my sister Becky, and my brother Chuck. His real name is Charles, but we call him Chuck. My real name is Jennifer and hers is Rebecca. We know who you are. You're Mrs. Beadle. Mr. Burdett told us."

Mrs. Beadle didn't say anything for quite a while, but

she took Jenny's hand and held on to it. Jenny looked even more scared, but she let her hold it. She could have got loose if she'd wanted to. Mrs. Beadle looked us over with eyes bright and shiny like a bird's, but almost hidden deep down in her wrinkles. She had more wrinkles than an old dried-up apple. Her hair was white, but there wasn't much of it. You could see the skin of her head through it. She had on black clothes, and she stood all bent over just like a witch, her left hand curved around the knob of a stick. Suddenly I guessed something, and forgot to be scared of her as I blurted it out. "It was you! The tapping! It was your stick, not a ghost message. You were walking around in the Ghost Wing when we—"

"So you were the ones," she said at last in that gray cobwebby voice. "And what were you doing in the—in my grandfather's study? Haven't people told you about how he can still be heard pushing back his chair from his desk and getting up and walking around in there?"

"There isn't any chair," Jenny whispered, her eyes wide and scared and her face white. "There isn't any desk."

"No, but you can hear it, just the same. They say."

"We thought it was old Jefferey, in the Ghost Wing—"

"They say he's there too."

Her voice was sort of making fun of "they," so I finally got up the courage to ask, "Is he, the one who

77

pushes back the chair, I mean—your grandpa, is he the one who was shot by the Yankees and is buried in the garden? Colonel Richard Winslow? Because if—"

"And you can see him sometimes out there too, in his Confederate gray uniform?" Jenny's voice was just a breath.

"Some can," Mrs. Beadle said. "Yes, he's the one. But don't you children know . . ."—and suddenly her eyes looked fierce instead of faraway, and she dropped Jenny's hand and rapped her stick hard on the floor—"that I don't allow anybody to come inside the gates? What are you doing here?"

"Then why don't you have a sign somewhere saying No Trespassing?" Chuck said reasonably, moving back a little so her stick couldn't reach him in case she decided to use it for hitting. Then he remembered his manners and added, "Ma'am? And we didn't come in the gates, we climbed over the wall."

"We were just interested," Jenny explained earnestly. "And anyway, don't you think it's nice to have visitors sometimes? You might like us if you knew us. I already kind of like you."

"You might invite us to lunch if you knew us," Chuck said wistfully.

Unexpectedly the old lady chuckled. It was the oddest sound, as rusty as if she hadn't laughed for years. Then she looked at me. "And what about you, young lady?" she said. "What have you got to say about it?"

I knew it was up to me, as the oldest, to apologize for all of us. I swallowed hard, and said, "Mrs. Beadle, I know we shouldn't have, and we ought to say we're sorry. But we wanted to explore, and a secret passage is such a—such a challenge. And he said there wasn't any way to get out of the priest's hole into the Ghost Wing, but—"

"He?" Mrs. Beadle asked. I wasn't going to tell on Arie, though. She might not let him hunt rabbits there any more, and his little brother and sisters might go hungry in the winter when the fishing wasn't too good.

"But there was," I went on shakily. "We found it. And then we heard the tapping and we didn't know it was just your cane. We were scared and ran, because ghosts might be around even in the daytime in a place that sort of belongs to them. We wanted to see them and yet we didn't—you know how you can want something and dread it at the same time? So we got out, fast, but it wasn't us who broke the window; the glass was already out. And then we got lost in the maze."

"And the path brought you right back here?" Mrs. Beadle chuckled again, as if to say it served us right. We didn't bother to correct her. "But then why did you come up to my door, if you were so frightened? Why didn't you just go home?"

"We couldn't. You see, we have something that belongs to you, and we had to bring it back. I found it under the floor in the priest's hole, and we read it while we were resting from running. It's very exciting—but it was your grandpa's, I guess; so we thought you ought to have it."

"And you had the courage to bring it to me." She pondered, not looking very fierce now. I handed the book to her, and she looked at it, but not as if she were really seeing it. "So that's how you knew his name."

"It's his diary—and he tells where he buried the Confederate gold!" Jenny piped up.

"Just part of it," I said.

"And we wanted to dig for it, but Arie doesn't want us to," Chuck said.

"Who is Arie?"

"Never mind," I said to Chuck. Then I told Mrs. Beadle, "Yes'm, that's right; it does tell about the gold. So we thought you ought to know. We wouldn't go digging for it unless you said it was all right."

"Remarkable," the old lady said. "Remarkable children. Whose children are you?"

"Sarge's cabin is over yonder," Jenny told her, waving in the general direction of it. "Where we're staying for the summer. Sarge is our grandpa. Our daddy and mama are Mr. and Mrs. Charles S. Dodd."

"Sit down over there, you children. You"—she pointed at me with her cane—"come sit here by me on the lounge. And read to me what you read in this book. My eyes are almost gone, and even with my glasses I couldn't see this writing."

I was sorry for her. Not to be able to see, not to be able to read books at all, would be just about the worst thing that could happen to anybody. "Yes'm, I'll be glad to." I sat down on the couch beside her. It was a slippery one with leather buttons. "But it's sort of a long story. And my little brother keeps saying he's very hungry—that's why he mentioned lunch a while ago, which wasn't very good manners—and we have our lunch basket hanging on a tree just outside your wall and, well, could we get it and let him eat while I'm reading?"

Jenny whispered to me and I said Aye and she whispered to Chuck and he said Aye; so she asked Mrs. Beadle—and Jenny can be very winning when she wants to—"Excuse me for whispering, but Mrs. Beadle, won't you have a picnic with us? Grandma put in four of everything, but Arie wouldn't come along when we said we were coming to see you. And there are peanut-butter-and-jelly sandwiches—so, please—"

"So Arie lost his nerve?" Mrs. Beadle smiled, and now I thought she looked much less like a witch and more like somebody's great-great-grandma. "But you three decided you had to bring back the diary. Remarkable. Yes, my dear child," she said to Jenny, "I think I'd like to have a picnic with you. I don't know when was the last time I had a peanut-butter-and-jelly sandwich. Or a picnic."

I asked Jenny, "Do you think you could find the

basket and come back here? You aren't scared now?"

" 'Course I could. 'Course I'm not scared. But Chuck'll come with me, won't you, Chuck?"

"Sure. Daddy told me to take care of you girls."

"All right. Hurry back. And I'll start reading the diary to Mrs. Beadle."

I wasn't a bit afraid of her now. The room we were in was unusual, but not scary. There was a huge wide mirror over the mantel, in a gold frame all carved and very beautiful.

She saw me looking at it. "It was Marie Antoinette's," she said. "You know who Marie Antoinette was?"

I nodded.

"My great-great-granduncle—" she went on.

"Old Jefferey?" I wondered; I didn't know I was thinking out loud until she sort of smiled and said, "His name was Geoffrey, spelled the English way: G-e-o-f-f-r-e-y."

"Oh."

"He brought many lovely things here from France and other places in Europe when he was building Winwood. That clock there, the furniture—and I have all the china, though I've had to sell some of the things." She looked sad about that, and I didn't blame her. The clock was a marvelous one with cupids holding up a golden ball with the face of the clock set into it. The mantel was black marble. "From Italy," she said, nodding at it. The fireplace had trash in it. There was an old-fashioned trunk open in front of it, with things strewn around as if she had been going through it and cleaning it out. There were some beautiful old-fashioned dresses made out of silk that seemed to be rotting and falling apart, and a silk patchwork quilt with faded feather-stitching around each block, and in the tray of the trunk, among other things (one was a feather fan!), I saw a pair of crumpled, yellowed old baby shoes. Suddenly I remembered she had had two children, and I remembered what had happened to them. I nearly started crying. How she must have felt when she came across those little old shoes. Probably the baby who had worn them was now the old man in the mental hospital. Or maybe they had belonged to the girl he killed when he lost his mind. I just had to sneak a look at the floor to see if the bloodstains that couldn't be scrubbed off were still there. I didn't see any dark spot, but the whole floor was pretty dark. Still, that was probably just some made-up story. Like the ghosts might be.

"Are there really ghosts here?" I asked Mrs. Beadle seriously.

She answered me just as seriously. "I suppose so. I think there are ghosts wherever there have been people who felt such strong emotions of love—or hate—that they couldn't die entirely when the body died. But I don't think the spirits of the dead can be seen or felt except by those who have some reason to remember.

There are ghosts here that I can see because they are my family. But I would see them even if they weren't here, even if I had no eyes. Perhaps I make them up in my mind; perhaps they are hallucinations, because I am very old and sad and I remember so many sad things that have happened here at Winwood. But you couldn't see them, because you are young and happy, and what was once at Winwood could mean nothing to you."

"Yes'm, I see. I think I almost see what you mean. But, other people—"

"They just make up those wild stories about the place because they haven't anything better to do. And because I won't have anything to do with them." She looked fierce again. "They never saw any of Winwood's ghosts, no matter what they say. They couldn't hear my grandfather push back his chair in his study. But I—I think I can. I can hear my great-great-grandaunt crying in the night because her lovely home is in such ruins. But perhaps it's only in my heart that she sobs like that."

"Yes'm," I said. I understood what she meant, in a way, but the hair prickled on my neck just the same. "But if we found the gold, you could fix up the castle just the way he planned to, old Jefferey—I mean Geoffrey—Mr. Winslow. And maybe she wouldn't cry anymore. Even in your heart," I added, feeling shy and not quite knowing how to say what I wanted to say.

"Bless you." Her chin dropped almost to her chest for a moment. Then she raised her head and said briskly, "So you found the secret passage, and the hiding place? I knew where it was, of course—I used to explore it when I was a child, with my brother." She didn't look as if she had ever been a child, somehow. It was sort of frightening to realize she had been, and now was so old. Would Jenny and I—? "He was killed quite young. Part of the old chimney out there collapsed on him," she went on, so low I could hardly hear her. "Oh, yes, this has always been a place of tragedy, my child. Every generation—tragedy, violent death."

The old Curse, I thought. The poison duel. "I'm— sorry."

"Well." She took a deep breath and shook her head as if she could shake the sadness out of her mind the way a dog shakes off water. "So you found where Grandfather hid from the Yankees? I'm not angry—you children aren't like the others, the ones who think I'm a witch." I felt ashamed, so I touched her hand, and then patted it a little. "But Jim and I never found any diary. There was a story in the family, of course, that Grandfather had brought home some of the Confederate gold, but we never knew for sure. That was supposed to be why his spirit was restless, because he had died without being able to reveal where he had hidden it. Jim and I used to hunt for it. We actually found the place where the family silver had been buried when

Sherman came through. It had been dug up after the War, but they had missed a few teaspoons. We were so excited when we found them. I still have them—the old silver pieces with the Winslow crest. But we never found the diary. How in the world did you—?"

"It was in between the floor and the beams," I told her. "I guess if you weren't looking at just the angle I was, you couldn't have noticed it, in the shadows that way, and covered with dust. But wait till you hear about the gold! Who was Eleanor, Mrs. Beadle? He said she would know where he buried it, under the Indian rock—that they had played there."

"That must have been my grandmother. Her name was Eleanor. They grew up together and were married quite young. They already had three children when he went to the War. She died of a broken heart, they said, soon after he was shot out there by the Yankees. If she knew about the gold, she never told anybody. But if she never found what he had written here, she probably never knew."

"He might have just buried it, that same night he got shot, and not had time to tell anybody—maybe that was why he wrote it down," I said. "He wrote in here how he buried it under that Indian stone where they played on the creek—" I began to read it to her. I read the last part first, about the gold, because it was the most exciting.

"So you children would like to look for it?" she said

when I had finished. "Well, I don't blame you. Jim and I would have looked even harder if we'd found the diary. I don't think you'll ever find the gold, though—nobody could possibly know now what he meant by the Indian stone—but you-all may look all you want. You have my permission." Somehow she sounded like Queen Victoria in the movie when she said that. "Because you had the conscience and the courage to bring the book to me."

"I'm glad we did," I said, "but we would've anyhow, even if we'd known you'd be mad at us and wouldn't let us hunt for the gold."

"That's why I'm giving you permission to look," Mrs. Beadle said. "But you'll come by here sometimes, won't you, and let me know how you're getting on with the search?"

"Of course we will," I promised. She looked as if she meant it, as if she'd really be glad to see us. Jenny was right; Mrs. Beadle was lonely and she did like having visitors, after all.

"Look, here they are with the basket." Jenny and Chuck were at the door, and I opened it. "Where'll we have the picnic?"

"In my dining room?" Mrs. Beadle suggested. "It's big enough—my great-great-granduncle meant for this wing to hold a reception room and kitchen and banquet hall once he got the big house built. This is the banquet hall, and the kitchen is huge." She got up and opened

the door into it, and we peered into a long room with
an enormous table and lots of heavy chairs. If it had
been round it would have been like King Arthur's
Round Table, with room for all the knights.

"I think maybe you're always supposed to have picnics
outdoors," Jenny said doubtfully.

"Well, how about the garden?" Mrs. Beadle tapped
her way to a side door and opened it. Her stick didn't

sound a bit like a ghost's fingers when it tapped along
now. We followed her outside, and there was the marble lady lying on her side, just as Mr. Burdett said, and
two marble benches that were as gray-and-green with
moss as the tombstone, and a place where there had
once been a fountain. "He was going to run water to
it in underground pipes from a spring higher up the
hill," Mrs. Beadle said. "Shall we sit here?" Weeds

grew up around the benches, but she pushed them aside with her stick, and we had the picnic right there, with Chuck sitting on the marble lady's hip. There were some tall black-green pointed trees that Mrs. Beadle said were Italian cypresses from Fiesole, Italy, and an immense spreading one that was yew from England. A few roses were blooming on bushes that had spread around among the weeds.

"Purple roses?" Jenny said. We had never seen any roses exactly that shade before, and they smelled sweeter than any of ours.

"They're rare old-fashioned ones from France—Cardinal Richelieu roses," Mrs. Beadle told her. She smiled at Jenny over her peanut-butter-and-crab-apple-jelly sandwich. I could tell she was having trouble eating it—she didn't have any teeth that I could see, and peanut butter does stick to the roof of your mouth—but she was making a good try. When she had swallowed at last, she said, "You know, dear child, you remind me of my little girl when she was your age."

For a wonder, Jenny didn't say "The one who—" and neither did Chuck. He was too busy eating. Jenny just ducked her head and said, "Thank you, ma'am," as if it were the greatest compliment—and I guess it was.

When we finished eating Mrs. Beadle wanted to give us a drink, but she didn't have anything in the house but wine and water. We took the water; the wine bottles looked awfully old and dusty, and I remembered the poison duel with wine and wished I could ask to see the wine glasses with the dregs still in them, but I didn't. The water was nice and cold, and I did ask if it came from the spring up the hill, but she said No— she had a well with a pump that her son had put in. She sort of caved in when she mentioned her son, and I was sorry I'd asked.

I could see that she was getting very tired now, probably because she was so old, and I thought it must be time for her nap. "I guess we'd better go now," I said, "but we'll come back and tell you about hunting for the gold, and if we find it we'll bring it right to you."

"Well . . ." She faltered. She seemed almost to have forgotten about the gold. I guess it was because she was so old, or maybe because she needed that nap.

"Please, ma'am, do you know where the creek is, where they played Indians?" Jenny asked.

Mrs. Beadle said, even more vaguely, "Oh, it's right out there. You know where the creek is, Nellie."

"Ma'am?" Jenny said.

"Nellie must have been her little girl," I whispered. "The one who's dead. She's confused now. Come on, we'd better go. Good-by, Mrs. Beadle, and thank you for letting us look."

Mrs. Beadle caught Jenny by the shoulder. Her hand

was almost as small as Jenny's and even skinnier—it looked sort of like a hen's foot. "Where are you going, Nellie?"

Jenny understood now. She said in her soothing voice, the one she uses to talk to Annabelle sometimes when the doll needs soothing, "Yes'm. It's all right. I'm only going with Becky and Chuck now. I'll come back. It's all right."

"Well—" Mrs. Beadle tapped her way to the door with us. We were already going down the steps, having said Goodby very politely, when suddenly Jenny turned around and went back and put her arms around Mrs. Beadle and kissed her on the cheek, and then ran back to us. The door closed.

"Why'd you do that?" Chuck asked, thumping the lunch basket against his knees as he walked. Boys don't understand things like what Jenny'd done.

"Because," Jenny muttered. She ducked her head and then said all in a rush, "Because she was crying. On top she was sort of believing, but underneath she knew I wasn't Nellie. She knows Nellie is dead, and it hurts her so much."

"She wasn't really crying. I'd have seen her crying."

"A little," Jenny insisted. "Inside, anyhow."

"She was just mixed-up, because she's so old," I told them. "People get like that when they're very old. Sometimes their minds are perfectly clear, like when she was talking to me while you two went for the lunch basket, and other times they get to wandering, thinking they're back in the past. She'll probably be clear again after she's had a rest. I hope she remembers us next time, and remembers that she told us we can hunt for the gold."

"Let's hunt right now!" Chuck said. He had eaten everything that was left of the lunch after we had had enough, and he was full of energy again. "Where do you suppose that creek is? And why did Arie act so funny about not telling us?"

We were walking past the tombstone now, and I wondered out loud why they had buried Colonel Winslow where he fell, and not in some family burying ground like most of the plantation houses had.

"His wife probably wanted him close," Jenny suggested. "If she died of a broken heart, she loved him terribly—"

"I bet she's buried here too," I said. "This could be the family cemetery—or close to it." We looked around, but if there were other graves nearby, they weren't marked, or the headstones had fallen and were hidden in the long grass. While we were looking, we found a little spring half-hidden in the underbrush, and a trickle of water flowed off from it down the hill.

"You don't suppose this could be The Creek?" Jenny said. "How big is a creek anyway?"

"Bigger than this," I said. "But when they were children, could they have called it a creek, just for their

Indian game? Do you see anything that looks like an Indian stone?"

We followed the little stream and turned over every rock that was anywhere near it, and Chuck caught some little black spring lizards that make good fish bait, for Sarge, and put them in an old can he found, and fastened his cowboy handkerchief over the top to keep them inside. But we couldn't see any rock that looked anything like an Indian.

"I don't believe this is the creek anyhow," I said. "It's just not big enough."

"But she said it was 'right out there'—as if it must be in plain sight and we couldn't miss it," Jenny argued.

"Well, if it's 'right out here' it sure is well-hidden," I said. "I don't know why that old Arie couldn't tell us—"

Just then Jenny said "Freeze!" and we all froze. In the quiet we could hear something rustle—louder than a bird—and then a crack, as if a foot had shifted on a twig. The underbrush was thick, and we couldn't see through the leaves, but I thought I could hear breathing. I knew it wasn't a ghost, but there are a few things that are even worse.

"Whoever's in there, come out!" I said loudly, as if I felt as brave as I sounded.

"Maybe it's a bear," Chuck said. "You wouldn't want a bear to come out."

Nobody came out, not even a bear. But I felt as though somebody was watching us. You know how it is when you know there are eyes watching you but can't tell exactly where they are? I get goosebumps on my arms and legs. Jenny whispered, "It might be her son who's escaped from the mental hospital and come back home to kill somebody else—"

"What a thought," I whispered back. Daddy says she has a vivid imagination. I wished she could imagine us out of this particular spot.

"Should we run?" Jenny breathed. "It might even be the will-o'-wisp—"

"Not in the daytime. But it might be a good idea to run anyway."

That was all it took. We were crashing through the underbrush and running for the road before you could say Scat! Chuck was doggedly hanging on to the lunch basket, though—probably because he remembered that it still had the four dimes in it that Grandma gave us for cokes, as well as his can of lizards.

When we stopped for a minute to rest—I had a stitch in my side—the noise didn't stop quite as soon; the crashing went on behind us for another moment. Jenny shrieked, "It's coming!" and took off. I grabbed Chuck's free hand and ran too.

The Mystery of the Indian Stone

Well, we lost it, or him, or whatever it was, when we reached the road, and we slowed down, panting. We went on to Mr. Burdett's store and got our cokes and told him somebody had been chasing us, but he didn't believe it. When we told him it was over by the wall that goes around the old Winslow place, he thought we were just imagining the Winwood ghosts. We didn't tell him we had been inside Wormwood. Jenny started to ask him about the creek, but I shut her up quick and rushed her and Chuck outside the store in time to preserve the secrets of the Fine-Brain Club.

"We've got to keep it all a Dead Secret," I told them while we started to walk back to the cabin. It always seems farther when you're coming back from an adventure. "If anybody knew about the gold, there'd be all sorts of people digging around here, hunting for it. We don't want any competition. They might not be willing for Mrs. Beadle to have it."

"Arie already knows about it," Chuck said, kicking at the basket with his knee but being careful not to bump out the can of spring lizards.

"Well, he'd better not tell! At least he doesn't seem to want to hunt for it," Jenny said.

I had a sudden horrid thought. "How do you know he doesn't? Maybe he just wanted to look for it on his own, without us along. Maybe he does know where there's a creek, with a rock that looks like an Indian's head. Maybe he wants all the gold for himself."

"He couldn't possibly," Jenny said positively. "That wouldn't be fair." She always believes the best about everybody. She doesn't even think a copperhead would bite her, not if she was nice to it.

"Anyhow, we've got to find the creek without him, and find the Indian stone before he can," I told them. "But let's not let anybody know what we're looking for. That would give it away. And don't tell Grandma and Sarge. They might tell us not to. All in favor say Aye." They did.

Grandma was kind of bothered about our clothes being so ragged and our faces so scratched. "Where in the world have you been?" she wanted to know.

"We went over and visited the old lady at Wormwood," I said airily. We believe in telling the grownups just enough to keep them satisfied, but not enough to upset them. Always the truth, of course, but not necessarily all of it. "She was real glad to see us, too. Yes'm, there are a lot of briars around there that tear clothes pretty bad. She had the picnic with us, in her garden. She thinks Jenny looks like her little girl used to look— sometimes she even thinks she is her little girl."

"Why, you shouldn't have bothered poor old Mrs. Beadle," Grandma said. "I thought you were going over to Mr. Burdett's."

"We did. We went there afterwards, to spend our money," I said. "And here's the change. Arie went home and didn't get a coke. But Mrs. Beadle is real nice, Grandma, after you get to know her. She's awfully old. You ought to go and see her sometime."

"She'd let you in if you told her you're our grandma," Chuck said confidently.

"Well, I hope you didn't disturb her," Sarge said.

"She liked being disturbed, after she got used to it," Jenny said. "She's lonesome, all right, but she didn't know she was. She invited us to come back. And I promised her we would. She knows I'm me, most of the time, but once in a while she does think I'm Nellie, her little girl. And Grandma, she's got purple roses in her garden."

"Maybe you can get me a cutting," Grandma said, laughing a little and looking at Sarge with the "I give up" look.

"I'll ask her," Jenny agreed seriously.

Sarge kidded us. "Did you see any ghosts?"

"You know ghosts don't come out in the daytime, Sarge," Chuck told him. "But a bear chased us."

"A bear?" Sarge raised his eyebrows. "I didn't know there were any bears closer than Brasstown Bald."

Grandma said, pretending to be mad, "So now it's a bear that tore your jeans!"

"Well, we didn't exactly see it, but it sounded like a bear when it started running after us."

"Becky?" Sarge turned to me for the answer.

"No, sir. I don't think it was really a bear. But there was something, or somebody, watching us in the woods. And it did come after us a little way."

"Sure it wasn't your imagination?"

I could tell Sarge was beginning to get upset, so I said, "Well, maybe we did imagine it. Wormwood is a kind of scary old place, you know. It could have made us nervous." I didn't want him getting alarmed about our safety and telling us not to go away from the cabin any more.

Sarge dismissed the subject. "Thanks for the fish bait, son. We'll catch us a big one with these fellows."

But Grandma still looked worried. "You children had better stay where I can see you, after this."

"Oh, Grandma!" Jenny protested.

"I mean it."

But Grandma got over being scared after a day or

two and let us off her apron strings again. Well, what really happened was that she got tired of having us always underfoot. We could go anywhere we wanted to if we'd promise to report in every three hours or at mealtimes, whichever came first, and to stay together at all times, and not talk to any strangers, and not ask to go out after supper. She let us make some cookies to take to Mrs. Beadle next time we went over there. Mrs. Beadle knew us all right, and didn't call Jenny Nellie but once. And she was glad to let us take some rose cuttings for Grandma.

We hunted over every inch of those woods for a creek somewhere near Wormwood, and there just wasn't any. We couldn't have missed it if there had been. It was maddening, because we knew Arie knew where it was.

"Gee Wiggles!" Chuck said. "I bet it dried up because there hasn't been enough rain."

"It rained pretty hard the night we caught Arie in the boat," Jenny reminded him. So much had happened it seemed a long time ago that we first thought of going to Wormwood, but actually it had been only a few days.

"There's something in Chuck's idea, though," I said. "Suppose something diverted the water, and where there was a creek then, there's only a dried-up creek bed now? Let's look for something like that!"

We had been looking for water, of course, so now

we had to start all over. We found several likely ravines that might have once held creeks. And there were plenty of rocks, but it would take a lot of imagination to see an Indian head in any of them. We dug deep holes under a few of them, the ones that might have shown a profile of the noble red man if his nose hadn't been broken off or something, but we didn't find a thing under them but more rocks. Sarge wanted to know why we were borrowing his fox-hole-digger so often. It's a handy little shovel that can also be a hoe if you turn the end down. It's rugged, but not heavy. It was just right for me to carry, and Jenny brought our girl scout ax and Chuck borrowed Sarge's smallest pick. "But what for?" Sarge wanted to know. "I don't mind as long as you don't lose them, but—"

"Have you forgotten about Jenny's rock collection, Sarge?" I asked, skillfully avoiding a real lie. "Maybe we'll dig up something good she can add to it. We found some fool's gold yesterday." We had, too, quite by accident. Jenny brought it to show him, looking eager and innocent. He was surprised that we knew what fool's gold was.

"They do say there's plenty of corundum in these hills," he said then, turning Jenny's rock over in his hand. "Maybe you'll find a ruby." He let us go without asking any more questions. I guess he figured we couldn't do much damage just digging.

We were working in a hole that had seemed more

promising than most of them because the rock over it was shaped like one of those things Indian women ground their corn in. When Jenny first noticed it, all rounded inside like a bowl, we were sure it was the Indian stone. We got so excited we could hardly dig. We were getting in each other's way, working so hard, and soon we were worn out and had to stop to rest. As we were lying flat on the edge of the hole, trying to catch our breath, I noticed the leaves of a bush on the other side of the narrow, dry creek bed quivering a little, although there wasn't even a bit of wind. "Freeze!" I whispered. "Jenny, see those leaves shaking, over there by that black-gum bush? Somebody's watching us again."

Chuck jumped up before I could stop him and grabbed up a rock and heaved it into the clump of bushes. It hit, and somebody hollered out.

"Gee Wiggles!" Chuck swore. "Got him!" He sounded mighty pleased with himself for a child who might have just riled a bear.

Of course, it turned out to be nobody but Arie Chance. He came out of the bushes with the rock in his hand, but he didn't throw it.

"So you're the one who's been watching us and chasing us," I said. "Looks like you could find something better to do."

"Who's watchin' and chasin' you? I got a right to set

a rabbit trap anywhere I want to that ain't posted. If I just happen to see you while I'm doin' it—Find anything yet?"

"None of your business," Chuck said rudely.

Jenny said regretfully, "You don't belong to the Club any more, Arie, so—"

But I wanted to find out something. "Arie, this is important. Wasn't it you who chased us the other day—that same day we got lost in the maze?"

"Chased you? Naw. I went on home. Did you really go to Old Lady Beadle's house?"

"We sure did, and she really liked us," Jenny bragged. "She gave us permission to dig for the gold, so there."

"Somebody was watching us, and ran after us when we were leaving," I told him.

"I been seein' you diggin' ever since then," he said, "while I was settin' my traps. You never seen me till now. But not that day. And I never have chased you."

I felt vaguely uneasy, even though I had decided there was no real danger in somebody's watching us in broad daylight. But now it occurred to me that if we should ever find the gold, the hidden watcher might try to take it from us.

"I wonder who it was, then?"

Arie wasn't about to be of any help. "Find any money yet?" he persisted. "Find out what that beckonin' light was?"

"No. But this one here is the best Indian stone yet," Jenny said, "I bet if we dig deep enough we'll find the gold right here."

"I don't think so, Jenny," I had to tell her. "This is already deeper than anybody would have dug to hide it. No, we'll just have to go on looking. Arie, why won't you tell us where the creek is? We'd take you back in the Club, and you could have a fourth of the reward if there should be any. We're hunting the money for Mrs. Beadle now, not for us."

"I can't fool around waitin' for any old reward. I got to get me a job that pays money," Arie said. He scowled. "My ma gets up before good daylight and works in the garden. She raises near 'bout ever'thing we eat, 'cept the fish and game I bring in. She already put up about two hundred jars of stuff for next winter, and she's hardly begun yet. Ever' day now she cans okra'n'-tomatoes. I bet we have okra'n'tomatoes runnin' out of our ears next winter. And we don't even like okra. But Ma says it's good for us. Then she spends all her spare time gettin' the yarbs out of the woods and fixin' 'em to sell. And she makes our clothes, and makes quilts to cover us, and does the washin' and scrubbin' and cookin', and she built us a hen house the other day, in case my uncle should give us some hens—but I helped her some with that. 'Tain't as if we had electricity, or water in the house. We got to bring all our water from the spring. It's the best spring in this county, but still—"

"Your mama does the washing without electricity—without a washing machine?" Jenny said. "For four children?"

" 'Course she does. Milly helps her, but Ma does the most of it. If I quit school and get a job, we can move to the old Roberts place where there's electricity and a pump. That's what we're goin' to do. But we'd have to pay rent over there. Ma gets our house now for nothin', just for givin' Old Man Settles garden stuff and washin' his clothes for him. It's on his place, you know. He lets us have firewood, too."

"Gosh," Jenny said. She was having a hard time imagining housekeeping without a washer and dryer. Grandma had them in the cabin even.

"Well, then, why don't you want to help us?" I said at last. "It might be enough so we'd get a big reward to split."

"No." He was abrupt. "And you better give it up. You'll never find it." He went off down the creek bed, kicking the rocks ahead of him and making a lot of noise.

"I wonder what's buggin' him," Chuck said.

"He can't stand for his mama to have to work so hard," Jenny said, frowning. "I don't think he really wants to quit school. I bet if they had enough money he'd like to finish high school anyhow."

"So why won't he help us and try to find the gold?" It was a real puzzle, and we couldn't think of a good answer.

Sarge took us up to Cherokee, North Carolina, for the Fourth of July weekend, to see the Indian village and the Indian play, *Unto These Hills*—all about The Trail of Tears, when the white settlers made the Indians leave their homes and go West. It was so sad that Jenny cried. It sure was a good thing he took us to Cherokee, because if I hadn't learned what I did up there we might not ever have found the Indian stone. But that was later.

During the drive home, while it was my turn to sit in front with Sarge, I asked him, "Sarge, did you ever see a will-o'-wisp?" Arie had mentioned it the day we saw him, and we had been noticing it some of the nights, still beckoning across the lake. So far we'd been able to ignore it, but in books there comes a time when the one who sees it can't resist it any longer.

"I don't think so," he answered. "Did you?"

"There's one across the lake from the cabin."

"No!"

"Really. There is. We can see it almost every night. Funny, though—there was one night we didn't see it. I'm not kidding; we do see it, Sarge. We haven't followed it yet, but—"

"And you won't. That's an order."

"Yes, sir."

"Show it to me tonight," he said.

"Yes, sir."

The big surprise came when we got back to the cabin. The lake had nearly disappeared! We'd only been gone a couple of days, but now we could barely see the edge of the water, way down to the right of the cabin. In front of the cabin was a neat little valley where the lake had been, and already there was some kind of soft green grassy stuff coming up all over it. The seeds must have been down in the mud all that time since last summer, Grandma said—a fast-growing weed.

"They tell me down at the store that they draw the water out of here to fill up the other lake, at Hiwassee, for boat races on the Fourth," Sarge said, beginning to unload the car. "But it would have gone down in a little while anyway. They dam the water up in the winter," he explained to us. "You know the big dam I took you to see when you first came? It's to prevent floods and make electric power. The dam backs the water up in here to form our lake. Then they let it out gradually, as they need it, when the rain-and-snow season is over, and the lake retreats from this end and leaves us a valley."

"Where do the fish go?" Chuck asked.

"They stay with the water if they know what's good for them. Fishing will be better at the edge of the lake now, everybody says, because there are more fish in less water. You can probably catch a big one now."

"Okay," Chuck said happily.

"Can we walk all the way across the bottom of the lake?" Jenny asked.

"Sure can," Sarge said. "But you might want to wait awhile—it may be muddy still."

"No—see, it's like a meadow. Anyhow, what's a little mud? I might find some good rocks that grew in the bottom of the lake!"

It was a fascinating idea, that we could walk where deep water had been. "Come on, Jen, I'll race you all the way across!" I said.

We dropped everything and raced pell-mell down the hill, Chuck after us, past the Becky-Jen where she sat high and dry, and across the green lake bed. I was ahead, of course; so I saw it first. I stopped so suddenly that Jenny nearly knocked me down—she was that close behind.

I shouted, not quite believing it yet, "Jenny! Do you see what I see?"

"Yes!" she shrieked. "You see it, Chuck?"

Hidden Creek

Chuck said, "I don't see anything but a—Gee Wiggles! It is! It's—"

"It's a creek!" I said. "That old Arie knew when the water went down there'd be a creek here. It was hidden under the lake all the time."

"Do you s'pose," Jenny said, "that Mrs. Beadle doesn't know that sometimes a lake covers the creek? She said the creek was 'right out there' and so it is, when the lake's not over it."

"I bet I know," I said. "I bet the creek's been there forever, but the lake hasn't. That creek was where Richard and Eleanor played Indian, all right. But the dam people backed the lake up fairly recently, probably not more than ten or fifteen years ago—"

"Twelve," Jenny said. "That's what Mr. Burdett said."

"And Mrs. Beadle hasn't been out much for so long

that she forgets the lake. She remembers the way it was when Nellie was a little girl."

"Whee!" Chuck shouted. "Gee Wiggles! We've found the creek! Now let's find the Indian rock."

There were enough rocks to make that seem hopeless. The bottom of the creek was covered with them, and there were big craggy rocks on the edges of it and flat rocks and thin rocks and reddish rocks and white rocks and gray rocks and greenish mossy ones. The creek itself seemed to come out of the side of where the lake had been, like an underground stream, and it curved and wandered, a pretty clear little stream, all the way across the lake bed. It was sunk so deep between its green banks that it wasn't even visible from the cabin porch. We named it Hidden Creek.

"I see minnows," Chuck said.

"I think they're tadpoles," Jenny told him. The two of them squatted at the edge of the water and dabbled at the tiny creatures. "See their little feet—"

"Come here!" I said sternly. "You two catch tadpoles some other time. Now we've got to hold an important meeting of The Club. We've got to figure out where that Indian rock is likely to be. We've got to think. Hard."

They came and sat down cross-legged with me on a big flat reddish rock that seemed just made for a council meeting. It had streaks of red and white, and Jenny said, "This one's so pretty I'm going to break off a piece

of it for my collection when we bring the pick down here."

"All right, but I wish it looked like an Indian," I said. "Do you see any markings on it that could possibly be an Indian face?"

We had to admit that none of them could be. "Meeting come to order," I said. "Do either of you Club members have a suggestion about how to go about this job? We're halfway to the gold, we've found the creek. Now—the Indian stone?"

"Brainstorming?" Jenny asked.

"Sure. Any wild idea?"

"Toss up an Indian-head penny and dig where it lands." Pretty good, for Chuck.

"Start over there where the creek comes out and dig under every rock that looks at all possible." That was my contribution.

"Walk the length of the creek first and look closely to see if there's any rock like an Indian and make notes of places to come back to and dig."

"That last is the best idea," I decided. "All in favor of doing what Jenny just said say Aye." We all voted for it. We went to the spot where the creek started from underground, and began walking along the bank. Pretty soon Chuck and Jenny took off their sneakers and were walking in the creek instead. I had to warn them to hang on to their shoes because they usually drop them somewhere. I was a little way behind them, looking at all the rocks more thoroughly than they were, when I heard Chuck say "Gee Wiggles!"

"What is it?" I rushed to them.

"Look! Somebody beat us to it!"

I looked where he pointed. There was no mistake. Someone had already been digging among the rocks on the creek bank. There was a deep hole with clay and rocks piled around it.

"That old Arie!" Chuck said, disappointed.

"Well, he didn't find it," I said consolingly. "Let him dig. You don't see any Indian face on these rocks, do you?"

"No, but—"

"Well, then! We'll go on looking until we find the Indian stone. But if you do see one that looks like it," I warned them, "don't say anything out loud. Just mumble the password under your breath and we'll wait until we're sure Arie's not watching us before we do any digging."

"What's the password, then?" Chuck asked.

"Oh, let's see—how about 'Huckleberry'?"

"Okay."

"Rats!" Jenny said. "There's the bell. Grandma's calling us just when we're about to find it!" Grandma had one of those big old farm bells on a post that she rang when she wanted us.

"Well, it does happen to be just about dark," I pointed out. "Tomorrow we can start early."

When we got back to the cabin, Grandma was talking to a lady with a little girl and a little boy hanging bashfully onto her skirts. "This is Mrs. Strickland," Grandma said. "Becky, Jenny, and Chuck, Mrs. Strickland. She wants to know if you've seen Arie anywhere."

"Why, no'm," I told Arie's mother. "We just got back from North Carolina, and we've only been playing out there a little while. We didn't see him anywhere."

"But we did see where—" Chuck started to say, but Jenny, who was closest, kicked him in time, and he remembered that the digging was a Dead Secret.

Jenny distracted Grandma's attention from why she might have kicked Chuck by putting on her innocent face and asking Mrs. Strickland what the children's names were.

"Bonnie, and this-un's Del," Mrs. Strickland said. "Speak to the little girl, Del." The kids both had almost white hair like Arie's, but they were much shyer. We all said Hello, but they didn't say anything. Jenny pulled some bubble-gum (unchewed) out of her pocket and untangled it from some cord and stuff and gave Bonnie and Del each a piece. They mumbled Thank you when their Mama made them. So they could talk, after all, when they wanted to.

"Well, I'll go on back," Mrs. Strickland said. "I'd give a pretty, though, to know where he's got to. We-uns ain't seen hide nor hair of him since good dark last night. He went fishin' and never come home. Like I told you. I knowed he played with your young-uns sometimes, so—"

"He'll probably show up when he gets hungry enough." Grandma tried to be consoling. "But if he doesn't come home soon, I believe I'd get the sheriff to look for him, if I were you."

"Yes'm. I reckon I will." But she didn't look too enthusiastic about that idea, and I remembered her no-count husband, who had broken the law and got himself killed. She probably didn't like even to think about sheriffs.

Sarge said, "And if I were you, I'd give him a good licking when he does come home." Our grandpa's bark is really worse than his bite. He's never hit one of us yet. But then, we never stayed out all night like that. I guess we'd better not try him too far.

"Law, he's not too big for me to whip yet!" Mrs. Strickland said. "I surely will whip him, if I can get my hands on him."

"Well, I hope he comes home soon," Grandma said. "I know how worried you must be."

"Yes'm, I sure am. And he didn't bring in my water, nor my stovewood neither." She started off, looking discouraged.

Grandma and Sarge said Good night, and we all did

too. " 'Night, Bonnie. 'Night, Del." They just ducked their heads and scampered off down the road without a word.

Mrs. Strickland answered, "Good night. You-uns come." I could have listened to her all night. The way Arie talked wasn't nearly so funny.

"Wonder where he is?" Jenny said. "You don't suppose he—"

"Huckleberry!" I said warningly, and she shut up. But I wondered too. He'd dug that hole last night— what if he had found the gold? And gone somewhere to do something with it before we could claim it for Mrs. Beadle?

The wind started blowing while we were eating supper on the porch, and Grandma said, "It feels like fall already, up here in the hills. Pretty soon we'll have to eat inside. The days are getting shorter, too. After June 21 the dark comes earlier and the sun rises later."

"The poplar leaves have already started turning yellow," Sarge remarked. "They're the first leaves to turn, except for the sourwood and black gum. Have you noticed?"

"I did!" Jenny said. "You mean those pretty bright-yellow leaves that look like tulips?"

"Yes."

"Gold," Jenny said. "Go-o-o-l-l-d-d—"

"Huckleberry," Chuck said.

"What, son?" Sarge asked.

"I just said Huckleberry," Chuck answered innocently.

"Funny. That's what I thought you said." Sarge grabbed him and rubbed his butch haircut. I figured it was time to get his mind on something else.

"Sarge, as soon as it gets dark, you can see the will-o'-wisp from here."

"I'd really like to see that. Strange I never noticed it."

It seemed as though dark would never come, just because we wanted it to. Grandma said, "Some folks around here call this 'the pink of the evening.' And some of them say 'dusk-dark.' Aren't those beautiful phrases? The mountain people do have a picturesque way of talking."

I put in, "Arie said he saw a snake one time that was 'all quirled round.' I thought that was funny."

"Coiled-and-curled, I guess." Grandma nodded. "It's a good word."

"Arie knows a lot, for a boy," I said, remembering some of the things he had told us while we were walking through the woods and around the lake to Wormwood that day. "He doesn't know much about things in books, but he knows which plants make dye—like joe-pye weed makes purple, and yellowroot makes yellow—and he showed us which leaves you use to make a poultice for your dog if he gets snake-bitten—"

"And he knows how to catch lots of fish and rabbits," Chuck said. "I wish we were still friends with him."

"Aren't you?" Grandma asked. Jenny and I both said "Huckleberry!" as quick as we could.

"Of course we are," I said, giving Chuck The Look. "Chuck just means he wouldn't help us dig. For rocks for Jenny," I added hastily. It's easy to give things away without thinking.

"He probably had some chores to do," Sarge said. "He has to help his mother, you know. He's the man of that family. I hope he comes home soon."

"I do hope nothing's happened to him," Grandma said.

"Oh, Arie can take care of himself," I answered carelessly.

The pink streaks had gone from the sky now and it was getting dark. Tonight was going to be a black night; the moon was covered by dark clouds. Last night up in North Carolina there had been a pretty, full moon.

We stared at the other side of the lake bed, but there was still no will-o'-wisp.

"If you children are going to stay out here in this wind, you've got to put on your sweaters," Grandma said. "You forget how quickly it gets chilly up here in the mountains once the sun goes down. This wind is cold."

"Yes'm." We put on our sweaters. Sarge was getting tired of waiting. He had filled his pipe twice, and I could tell he was just about to go in and look at television. Then Jenny said, her voice all excited, "There it comes! See it, Sarge?"

Sure enough, the wavering light had come out at last, faint and yellow. It was beckoning again, forward and back, appearing to come a little closer and then retreating. I shivered, and it wasn't the chilly night that made me cold. I had understood, in a way, what Mrs. Beadle meant about the ghosts at Wormwood, but she hadn't explained the will-o'-wisp away.

Sarge said with interest, "It's odd, all right. Yes, it does appear to be moving, doesn't it?"

"Beckoning," Jenny whispered. "It wants us to follow it and get killed—in quicksand or over the edge of a cliff—"

"Nonsense," Sarge said. "There's no cliff over there, and if there's any quicksand, nobody ever warned me about it. Funny, though. I can't figure out why a light should be moving just that way, a little bit forward and then wavering and seeming to retreat—"

"You aren't scared of it, are you, Sarge?" Chuck said confidently.

"No. Are you?"

"No. 'Course not. Only—"

"The thing to do," Sarge said, "when you see something you can't explain logically, something that appears to be supernatural, is to investigate."

"Now, Franklin," Grandma protested, "you know

they mustn't do that. They're altogether too curious as it is. Don't go telling them to be more reckless than they already are, for goodness' sake."

"I mean, with an adult, of course," Sarge said. He looked at us, all three sitting in the hammock, gazing first at him and then at the will-o'-wisp, and nursing our goosebumps. "How would you like," he said tantalizingly, "to walk across there right now with me and just see what it is?"

The Mysterious Will-o'-wisp

I could feel Jenny shivering and I knew there were goosebumps on top of my goosebumps. But of course we wanted to. It's such a delicious feeling to be all keyed-up and scared and expecting something out of this world to happen, and yet to know there's somebody big and solid like Sarge to keep anything really dangerous from harming you though you're right on the edge of it.

"Will you take your gun?" Chuck asked Sarge. "I kinda wish you'd take your gun, Sarge." Chuck always wanted him to take the gun. He was always hoping for a bear for Sarge to shoot so as to make him a bearskin rug for his room at home.

"Silly," Jenny told him. "Guns aren't a bit of good

for shooting will-o'-wisps. You can't shoot something that isn't real."

"Maybe you could with a silver bullet." That was the way it was with vampires, I remembered. "Have you got any silver bullets, Sarge?"

"Not a one," Sarge said cheerfully. "But we'll take the gun along anyhow, to please Chuck. Just in case we meet a bear over yonder." He was kidding, and he didn't load the gun. I guess he was afraid somebody might be shot accidentally; so many people are. But he put some bullets in his pocket. "Don't you want to bring your gun too, boy?" he asked Chuck.

"Sarge, you know my gun won't really kill anybody."

"Mine won't either," Sarge said. "Not if I can help it."

"You got a medal in the war."

"That was different." Chuck was always bragging in school about Sarge's World War II record. But his medal was for sharpshooting, not for fighting. He was in the medics and never killed anybody at all.

We were very quiet as we went across the lake bed, half-holding our breath as we kept close behind Sarge. He walked as if he might be scouting in enemy territory, I thought, being cautious yet not afraid. He didn't really think it was anything supernatural, I could tell; he was simply curious. And he was going to be careful until he found out just what it was.

When we came to the creek he waded across first,

boots and all, to see how deep it was. It came only to his knees in the deepest part, and it wasn't very wide, but he carried us across it one at a time because we might have cut our feet. His boots squished water when we started walking again, but he took them off and got them a little drier by shaking and wiping, so that he could at least walk without being heard.

We reached the other side of the lake bed without seeming to get much closer to the will-o'-wisp. Now we climbed the bank and were nearly to Wormwood. "Must be an optical illusion," Sarge muttered. "We ought to be getting closer to it."

"Sir?" Chuck said.

"An optical illusion is something that you think you see but don't really. Or at least, you don't see it as it actually is."

"Well, we all see this, so it's not an illusion," I said.

"But maybe it's actually different from the way we see it," Jenny put in.

"That's what I mean," Sarge said. "It appears to be a moving light, and back there it appeared to be coming toward us and then going back. Actually—" He stopped and stared into the dark as if he had X-ray eyes. "Becky," he said in a different tone, "are there any houses over here? Besides Winwood?"

"Yes, sir. Well, not houses exactly. Down at the back of the castle there are some old falling-down shacks like barns or chicken houses or something. And there's one that might have been a slave cabin or a servant house—"

"That's it!" Sarge said softly. "There's a light in that house."

"But why does it move like it was beckoning?"

"If you look carefully, you can see why." Sarge always wanted us to think for ourselves. He made us figure things out instead of telling us. But this one he had to explain. I looked carefully, but I couldn't see the reason. The brick wall had tumbled down on the lake side and there was nothing but trees and stuff between us and Wormwood, and now that he mentioned it, the light did seem to come from where the old shack was, below and behind Wormwood. But it still seemed to be moving as if it were looking for something, though as we got closer and closer the effect wasn't quite like that after all.

"I guess it's not really moving," Jenny said. "Like it's an optical illusion."

"That's right; the light's not moving," Sarge said. "It's the trees in front of it that are moving. See? The light is coming from a window or opening in that shack. Ordinarily the tree branches are so thick in front of it that they hide the light from view. But there's an opening over there where there aren't any leaves—a kind of hole between the branches—and on a windy night the thick branches are blown away from in front of the light so that it shows. The wind blows the branches back and forth in such a way that the light appears and disappears, and the next time the wind blows it seems to be in a different place, as if it were wavering and beckoning. See? Think back. Wasn't it always on a windy night that you saw it, and on still nights that you didn't?"

I thought back, and he was right. "I get it!" I said.

"I do too," Jenny announced.

"There's always a logical explanation for things that seem supernatural," Sarge said, sounding sort of satisfied with himself, "and if you investigate, you can usually find it."

"I know," Chuck said. " 'Let that be a lesson to us.' " He was quoting Grandma.

"Then we've still got to find another logical explanation," Jenny said, shaking her head and frowning. "On account of why is there a light in Mrs. Beadle's old servant house at all? She hasn't got any servants. They'd be scared to stay there even in the daytime."

There shouldn't have been, of course. Sarge gave Jenny credit, afterward, for good thinking. Now he just stood quite still for a minute and then said, "You're right. I want you children to go back to the cabin while I creep over there and look into that."

"We want to look too!" Jenny said. "We won't make any noise. We can be quieter than Indians."

Sarge must not have thought it was dangerous, or he wouldn't have let us. He said later that he had thought it might be just a tramp or some squatters, and he felt able to protect us from such people. Anyhow, he let us come. "Not a sound," he warned us.

The window was well hidden by the trees, and if it hadn't been for that hole in the branches that the wind opened up, nobody would ever have seen the light. Mrs. Beadle was careful not to let anybody on her place, and since she didn't get around outside much, 'specially after dark, she couldn't possibly have guessed that anybody was there.

We sneaked up to the window; it was low enough so that even Chuck could see in. The glass was cracked and real dirty—I was surprised that it had any glass at all. Somebody must have fixed it up for a servant to live in—later than slavery times, but not very recently.

I got only one glimpse though, before Sarge was motioning us all back. I knew why, because of what I'd seen through the window. There was a man in there, and he looked like a tramp, all right. He hadn't shaved in ages, much less washed. But it wasn't only the way he looked. What made us gasp was that he had Arie Chance in there with him, and he was holding Arie prisoner! What they call a hostage in TV plays. I knew Arie was a prisoner because his hands were behind his back and he was sitting against the wall with his feet

tied. There was plenty of light to see them by, but it all came from a bright fire in an old country fireplace. No wonder the will-o'-wisp seemed to waver.

When we had all retreated far enough away into the trees, Jenny whispered, "We've got to rescue him!"

Sarge said, "Right. But not by ourselves. How fast can you guys run?"

"Pretty fast," Chuck said. "But Sarge, you've got a gun. You could capture the man—you're not scared?"

"Discretion is the better part of valor," Sarge told him. "Never tangle with a criminal if you can get law officers to do it for you. It's their job. That man probably has a gun, too. If I had to shoot it out with him, I would. But since I don't have to, it's more sensible to get the sheriff or the state troopers to do it. They know more about capturing criminals than I do. And I have to think about you children and your safety."

"What about Arie?" Jenny said worriedly.

"Arie's in no immediate danger. If he were, of course I'd go in and try to save him. But if the man intended to hurt him, he wouldn't have bothered to tie him up like that. No, he's holding Arie for some reason, but nothing will happen to him before we can get the sheriff. Now you guys run for the cabin as fast as you can, and tell Grandma to phone the sheriff and the state troopers and send them here as quick as they can come. Go on now."

Chuck and Jenny ran. I said, "What about you, Sarge?"

"I'm going to stay outside the place and keep an eye on him until the sheriff gets here. Just in case."

"I want to stay with you," I said.

"Nothing doing. You'll be helping more if you hurry back and see that the kids get the message right. If the sheriff didn't realize that he had to come right now—or if he couldn't tell exactly where it is he's needed—you see? So hurry, Becky!" He was putting a bullet in his gun while he told me.

"Yes, sir," I said, and I ran so fast I got there as soon as the others did.

Grandma actually turned pale when we told her. She grabbed Chuck and held him, even while she phoned, as if she thought the tramp might get him yet and tie him up with Arie. Chuck squirmed and wiggled himself loose from her. Grandma managed to give the sheriff the facts, and then put me on the phone to tell him just where the shack was. I wasn't exactly calm, either, but I did tell him where to go, and about Arie and all, and that Sarge was standing guard, and that he'd said to hurry, please. Then while Grandma was calling the state patrol, Jenny and Chuck and I slipped out and ran, before she could tell us not to, back across the lake bed on the double, splashing right through the creek without even noticing it.

"What are you-all doing here?" Sarge whispered when we found him. He was still on guard among the trees, where he could see the shack without being seen. "You know I meant for you to stay there once you got there."

"You didn't say we had to. We got the sheriff. Grandma's calling the state patrol," we reported. "She didn't exactly tell us not to come back, either. Oh, please let us watch, Sarge! We never saw anybody get arrested before. Or rescued, either, like Arie's going to be. We'll keep way back out of the way—"

He wouldn't have let us, of course, except that right then the sheriff came up with several other men, slipping quietly through the trees, and things began to happen so fast that Sarge just shoved me behind him and held Jenny and Chuck each by one arm while he explained it all in a hurry, and then stood back with us while the Sheriff—his name is Mr. Jenkins—crept up to the window and looked in. He beckoned to the other men and put one by the window and sent one around to the other side and took one with him. He went up to the door and pushed it in, real sudden, to take the man off-guard. We listened for shots, but it was quiet—we couldn't even hear their voices, at that distance. A cricket was chirping loud somewhere near us, and that was all we could hear.

"Rats," Jenny whispered disgustedly. "They aren't going to shoot it out."

"You ought to be glad," I said, though I felt a little

bit disappointed too. "Arie might get hit. Think how his mama would feel."

"I guess you're right," Jenny muttered. "That old tramp—I bet he was the one chasing us that day. See, he wanted to scare us away from Wormwood so we wouldn't go poking around any more and see that he was hiding out in this shack."

"Hush!" Sarge said.

The door of the shack opened and Sheriff Jenkins came out, pushing the tramp ahead of him kind of rough. They had their flashlights on now, and we could see. Arie was next, and the deputy, Mr. Banks, had his hand on Arie's shoulder. Sarge relaxed then and went over to talk to them, knowing we were safe. I thought I heard Sheriff Jenkins tell Sarge, "He's the one— murder and robbery—"

We rushed over to Arie, naturally. "How'd he get you? How come he didn't keep you for a hostage and make them let him go to save you?"

"Aw, he didn't have no gun," Arie said. "If I'd a had any sense he wouldn't have caught me, neither. But he jumped me when I wasn't lookin', and he's bigger'n me and he got me tied up and I couldn't get away."

"Why did he want to keep you, then, if it wasn't for a hostage?" Jenny asked. "Looks like he'd rather not've been bothered with a prisoner while he was hiding. Say, why was he hiding there in that shack anyway?"

"He didn't want me," Arie told her. "He just wanted to make me tell him what I did with—" And then he stopped. "I got to tell that sheriff something," he said. "Leave me go, now."

"What you did with what?" Jenny jumped up and down, she was so excited.

Shaking her off in order to get to Sheriff Jenkins, Arie said over his shoulder, "With the gold money."

The Clue to the Treasure

I was stunned. Jenny said to me, "He found it—" and her mouth quivered like she was about to cry. "How could that have been the Indian rock—where he dug the hole—and we didn't see it . . . ?"

"Come on," I said. "We'd better hear what he tells the sheriff." We moved in closer.

"We tried," Jenny said. "Mrs. Beadle's got to believe we tried."

Arie was talking earnestly to the sheriff, and the sheriff was listening hard.

"Let me get this straight, son," he said at last, as if he was absolutely too astonished to believe his own ears. "You want to give the college back the gold coins your pa and Bynum Watson here stole—"

"Not Pa," Arie said, his voice shaky. "He was drivin'

Mr. Watson's car that night, but he didn't know what Mr. Watson was doin' in that college buildin' until afterwards. He thought Mr. Watson was seein' one of the teachers about sellin' him a coon-dog pup. Ginger had a new litter—we were goin' to get one of 'em too. I heard Pa when he told Mr. Watson he better take the gold money back to where he got it. I reckon that was why he killed Pa."

"I recognized Watson here the minute I saw him," Mr. Banks told Sheriff Jenkins. "Didn't you, Foy?"

"Sure did. And that reward's still posted. Murder and robbery." Sheriff Jenkins turned to Arie. "Your pa was J. D. Chance," he said, as if Arie didn't know. "It was about five or six years ago. I remember it was hog-killin' time—November—"

"Yes, sir," Arie said. I punched Jenny. It didn't sound like the right gold money.

"You must have been only about nine or ten," the Sheriff said to Arie.

"Yes, sir. Nobody'd believe me when I told 'em Pa wasn't in on it. Even Ma wouldn't believe me."

"You weren't there when he killed your pa, were you, son?" Mr. Banks said kindly. "How'd you know—?"

"Mr. Watson dropped Pa off when he druv by here that night, but later on Pa said he was goin' to walk over to the Watson place—'twa'n't far—to get him that coon-dog pup Mr. Watson had promised him. I wanted to go too, to help pick out the pup, but Pa said No, that I ought to be in bed. So I went to bed, but after he left I climbed out the window and skinned down the chinaberry tree and took out after him, aimin' not to let him see me. He didn't neither, but I caught up with him and stayed out of sight. I couldn't wait to see our pup. Never did get him, though.

"There was a lantern lit in the shed, and Mr. Watson was in there solderin' up a box, and when he shifted it I could see gold money in it. Pa said somethin' to him and he said No, he wasn't goin' to give it back, neither. I sneaked in closer, and heard Pa arguin' with him about it, tellin' him he had to give it back, that anyhow he couldn't get nothin' out of it—he couldn't spend that kind of old-time money without people noticin'. But Mr. Watson said he could get at least twenty thousand dollars for them if he sold ever' one of the coins separate. He only had to hide 'em for a few years, he said, till it was safe to bring 'em out one at a time and sell 'em like that. He said he'd cut Pa in on it if he'd keep his trap shut. Pa said he didn't want nothin' to do with it, that he'd only just caught on to what Mr. Watson was really doin' at the college that night, and he wished he hadn't never heard of Ginger's pups nor gone over there with him neither.

"Mr. Watson kept tellin' Pa to shut up or he'd be sorry. He said he hadn't really planned the job when he went over there, but it was too good a chance to pass up. Pa said he'd give him one more chance to take the stuff back before Pa went to tell the sheriff. I reckon that was where Pa made his mistake, because Mr. Watson told him he was already in it whether he wanted to be or not, that ever'body who seen 'em together over at the college would think Pa helped steal the coin collection, and that the best thing Pa could do would be to help him bury the stuff and make a getaway before it was missed, because he knowed they'd be suspected. Pa pretended to give in to him then, but I knowed he was just goin' along with him to find out where he buried the stuff so he could tell the sheriff where to find it. But Mr. Watson must've caught on and killed him so there wouldn't be nobody alive who knowed where it was but him. Anyhow, he put his pick and mattock in his car and they druv off with the box. That was the last time I seen Pa alive. I went in the shed and looked at Ginger and the pups by myself, and picked out the one I'd like to've had, and patted it on the head a little bit, and then I went on back home and climbed up the chinaberry tree and got in bed. It was mornin' before Ma told me Pa hadn't come home. I was scared then that somethin' had happened to him, and it had. He was dead."

Bynum Watson muttered, "I didn't plan to kill J.D. I thought he was gon' to run away with me, till after we got the stuff buried and started drinkin' moonshine. I was drunker than he was so I let him drive the car. He started toward town instead of gettin' away, so I caught on that he was about to turn me in and show Foy where we'd buried the coins. I hit him on the head with a bottle and pulled him out of the car and then started hittin' him with the mattock, and before I knowed what happened he was dead. And I heard a car comin' and had to run for it or be tried for murder. So I figured the stuff was safe where I'd buried it and after the fuss all died down in a few years I could come back and get it and sell the coins one at a time. That's what I was doin' now—but I had to hide out until the lake went down so I wouldn't be recognized and arrested. If it hadn't been for that little runt—" He looked so vicious that I was glad there was a deputy on each side of him to keep him from jumping on Arie.

"You got it away from him somehow?" Sheriff Jenkins said to Arie. "How in the world—? There's a pretty nice reward for the return of that coin collection."

"It wasn't for no reward that I wanted to find it," Arie said. His face looked real pale in the dim light from the flashlights, all pointed at the ground. He looked like if he hadn't been a boy he might have been crying. I saw his Adam's apple move up and down when he swallowed; his neck was so skinny. He went on, "My Pa, he wasn't no mean guy. He took me fishin' all the time, and once he bought me a knife I wanted real bad, and he learned me how to shoot squirrels with his own gun. I felt awful when he got killed like that. Mr. Watson got away, but my pa was dead, and folks all thought he deserved it. Even Ma wouldn't believe he wasn't no thief. So I thought if I could find that valuable gold money and give it back and tell people it was because Pa wanted it gave back, they wouldn't think so bad of him no more. And maybe Ma wouldn't neither. She's hard on him now when she talks about him."

"So all the time—" the Sheriff said.

"All this time I been lookin' for it. I must've dug in a million places. But I wasn't even warm until—" He looked at us kids and I guess he remembered how he swore not to tell the secrets of the Fine-Brain Club, even if he wasn't a member any more. So he just said, "Until somethin' made me think what a good hidin' place the edge of the creek would be. Because if you buried a tight box there when the lake was down—in November—and marked the place with some certain kind of rock so you could tell where it was, the lake would hide it for a long time ever' year, and nobody would think of lookin' for it in the bottom of the lake. I'd always been afraid Mr. Watson would come back for it before I could find it, and I kept watchin' for him while I was huntin'. And I bet he did mean to kill my pa, too, so there'd be nobody but him knowin' where the gold money was hid."

The prisoner was looking at Arie as if he could kill him as well now, and I shivered, and Jenny whispered, "Isn't it just like on TV!"

The Sheriff said, "Then, Arie, how'd you find out where to look for the coins?"

"The kids told me about seein' a light over here, and I figured if Mr. Watson did come back for the stuff he buried and happened to get here before the lake went down, and had to wait, this'd be a real good hideout. I sneaked close and watched, and sure enough I seen him, but he never seen me." He looked at us and grinned, but it was a friendly grin. "I let the kids think it was a ha'nt, over here, to keep 'em from goin' near the shack, because I didn't want nobody to catch him until I'd seen where he went to dig for the gold money. It wasn't till last night that he slipped down there and started diggin'. I reckon he'd been waitin' ever since the lake went down for a good moonlight night, so he wouldn't need any light, because all he had was lightwood knots in the shack."

"Go on about the coin collection, kid."

"Well, I could just barely see him from where I was, and I snuck as close as I could get without him seein' me. He didn't have nothin' to dig with but an old broke piece of a rake that he'd picked up somewhere, and after a while he was havin' so much trouble with the rocks that he went away to hunt for somethin' else to dig with. I reckon that was what he went for. I had my pickax and so I hurried down there and pried up the rocks without makin' too much noise."

"And you found it?" The Sheriff sounded as if he could hardly believe it.

"It was right there," Arie said. "The old box was rusted, but I bet the water didn't get in, he had soldered it so good. I didn't have time to open it. I made haste and hid it the best I could, way off under some leaves and stuff. But then I made my big mistake. I come back to see if there was anything else in the hole. And I wasn't keepin' an eye out for him like I ought've, and he got me."

"But you didn't tell him where it was—?" I breathed. "He tortured you for a whole day and night and you didn't let on where the box was."

"Aw, he didn't do nothin' to me," Arie said. "We were pretty hungry—we didn't have nothin' to eat but some roastin' ears he stole out of a field. But he didn't do nothin' but tie me up so I couldn't get away, and keep askin' me where I hid it, and tellin' me about what all we could do with it if I'd come in with him."

"You were his only chance to find the coins," Sheriff Jenkins said. "Lucky for you you didn't tell. He might have killed you after he found out where you hid them. And if these folks hadn't investigated the light, he just might've lost patience with you and done a whole lot more to you than he did."

He told Banks to take Bynum Watson back to the car while Arie uncovered the coin collection.

I was afraid Sarge would want to go back to the cabin then, but he was too interested. We tagged along, and Arie led the way to where he had hidden the old box among the trees and covered it with underbrush. He dragged it out and handed it over to the sheriff, kind of proudly, and I didn't blame him for being proud. Sheriff Jenkins said, "Thank you, Arie Chance. I'll see that you get credit for this. The newspapers will make a big story out of it. And I'm sure that reward's still good."

Arie stood a little straighter and held his head up and said, "Give my pa the credit, please, Mr. Jenkins. For wantin' it gave back. I just had to find it and turn it in for him because he couldn't do it himself. Ma says the only way we can ever amount to anything is to do what's right. And I figured that was what was right. Pa did too."

Sarge said, "Good for you, Arie!"

But Jenny teased him. "What your Mama's going to do to you, for staying out all night!"

"Aw, she won't do nothin'."

"She said she was going to whip you. She was worried about you and asked us if we'd seen you."

"She don't really hurt when she whips me."

"I guess I can explain it all to Mrs. Strickland so she won't punish Arie," Sarge said, smiling. And he did. The last we saw of Arie that night, he was sitting at their table with an old oil lamp lighted on it, and eating a piece of summer-apple pie. His mama offered us some, too, but Sarge said we didn't have time, thank you; we had to get back and let Grandma know everything was all right, because she'd be worried about us. I was sorry we were in such a hurry, because it looked like awfully good pie.

Sure enough Grandma had worried about our going back over there, but she couldn't really blame us. We told her all about it, and it sounded more exciting than a TV show by the time we got through telling it. "And we were the ones who gave Arie the clue!" Jenny bragged. "We told him about the light, and that tipped him off that Bynum Watson was hiding at Wormwood, so he could watch and catch him digging—"

"Yes, and pretty soon that murderer might have hurt Arie, if we hadn't gone over there to see what the light was, and then got the sheriff and helped capture him," I added.

"You know," Jenny said thoughtfully, "I never did think it was a real will-o'-wisp." That's what Sarge calls hindsight.

Grandma told Chuck, half teasing, "I was counting on you to stay and protect me, and you went off too, playing cops and robbers—"

"Aw, gee, Grandma!" He put on his exasperated look. It's a real comic look. "Gee Wiggles! Why didn't you want the girls to stay, too?"

"We're older," Jenny said without too much logic.

It was pretty late when we got to bed. We kept on talking about everything, even after we were supposed to be asleep, and of course Jenny had to bring Annabelle and Huck up to date on the whole thing. Grandma had to call to us two or three times to hush up and go to sleep.

When I thought both the others were finally sound asleep, Jenny said from her bunk softly, "Becky? You know what? I guess the reason Arie didn't want us to dig was because he was afraid we might accidentally find those rare coins instead of the Confederate gold, and then he wouldn't be able to do what he wanted to do for his pa."

I had actually forgotten about the Confederate gold! That's what somebody else's adventures can do to you.

"So," Jenny went on, "maybe we could let him be in the Club again?"

"We'll take a vote on it in the morning," I said. " 'Night, Jen."

But in the morning I had something more important to think about. Because as soon as I woke up, before daylight, I saw the thing that gave me the clue. And all of a sudden, I knew absolutely certainly where the Indian rock was!

The Lost Gold of the Confederacy

I had to get up to go to the bathroom, and I was careful not to wake the others. I took Chuck's flashlight to see my way without turning on the light. We always did that because we had to go through Grandma and Sarge's room.

When I came back I looked at the clock. It was five o'clock, and still kind of gray outside and dark inside. Then the flashlight's beam just happened to stray onto the clothes we had taken off, and I noticed that the seat of my white shorts was red, and the seat of Jenny's yellow shorts was red, and the seat of Chuck's blue pants, even, looked kind of rusty. I stood there looking at them, trying to remember what it was that was beating at my brain, that I knew I ought to remember right then, because it was so important. It was a clue. Definitely. It was something I needed to remember. And I couldn't put my finger on it even though I was right on the edge of knowing. It had something to do with the red on those shorts.

I climbed back up to my bunk and lay there trying to think what it was. I had nearly fallen asleep again, when—click! Just like that, it came to me.

Indian red! That's what it was!

I had read about Indian red in the booklet Sarge had bought for us in the Indian village at Cherokee. I always knew that everything I ever read would come in handy some day, but I couldn't know how soon I'd be able to use that bit.

Indians used the red stuff as war paint—or to paint their faces for ceremonial dances. It came from an ore—and an ore was a rock.

I climbed down again and took the flashlight and got the dictionary and carried it into the bathroom to read what it said: "Indian red: a yellowish-red iron ore, native iron (ferric) oxide, used by North American Indians as war paint."

Now it was all clear as day to me. That big flat council rock we had sat on had reddish streaks. They were the iron oxide that the Indians had used for war paint! The children Richard and Eleanor somehow knew about that, and probably painted their faces with it playing Indian, and called it the Indian stone! We had actually been sitting on the gold that very day. I knew it in my bones as surely as I ever knew anything. I never felt so excited in my life and I rushed back to the sleeping porch.

"Wake up, Jenny!" I whispered. I went over and shook Chuck by the shoulder.

Jenny said sleepily, "What's the matter? Did he get away?"

Chuck grumbled, "Gee Wiggles! I just got to sleep—"

"Come on, both of you!" I commanded. "Up and out! Get dressed, quick! Sweaters—it's chilly. The password for today is GOLD!"

They both sat straight up. "Gold? What do you mean, Beck?" They began to dress as fast as I was dressing.

"I know where the Indian rock is! I know for sure that's the one!" I told them.

"Which one is it? Have we seen it?" Chuck stuttered with excitement—or maybe his teeth were chattering; it was so cold.

"How d'you know? How can you be sure?" Jenny urged.

"I remembered something." I would tease them a little. Just a little, because I was dying to tell them. I couldn't even wait to make them figure it out for themselves, the way Sarge does.

"What? Becky, tell us!"

"We were sitting on the Indian stone yesterday! Right on top of Colonel Winslow's bags of gold."

"How do you know?"

"See these shorts we were wearing? See the red on them? Remember the booklet about the Indians that Sarge bought us at Cherokee—the section where it told about painting their faces for ceremonies? And war paint? The Creeks used more war paint than the Cherokees though, I guess. Remember the 'war pots'? Stones that had red stuff in them that the Indians rubbed on their faces? That's what we were sitting on, a stone full of war paint! And I just know, somehow, that Richard and Eleanor used it for war paint when they played Indian, and so that was what they called their Indian stone!"

"You could be right," Jenny said. "Let's go!"

"Wait for me," Chuck said, trying to get the knots out of his shoelaces. We waited. "Are we going before breakfast?" he asked.

"Sure we are! It's only just after five o'clock. We can't possibly wait until after breakfast."

We hurried to get the digging tools and were careful not to make any noise that would wake the grandparents. Then we raced across the lake bed to the creek. As we ran I couldn't help saying, even if I was panting and out of breath and had a stitch in my side, "Well, Arie may know more about what plants to make dye from than we do, but he didn't know about Indian war paint! Because he doesn't read. You see, Chuck, you've got to be reading all the time you aren't doing something else!" Chuck just grunted. His grunt meant that he's usually doing something else. He doesn't absorb too well when I point a moral. Jenny already likes to read; so I didn't need to say anything to her.

Dawn is a nice time of day—almost as nice as twilight. It's gray, too, but fresher. Twilight is like gray velvet, soft and warmish. Morning is silver, Jenny said once, sharp and keen and cool to touch. When we arrived at the large flat rock with the red streaks, there was just a bit of red in the sky to the east too. "Indian red!" Jenny shouted. It did look just about the same color.

This was the big moment. Was the gold under the rock or wasn't it? If it was there, nobody had touched it for over a hundred years, not since Colonel Winslow had put it there and died before he could get back to it. We all felt how solemn a moment it was. I put the edge of the pick under the rock and heaved. It stirred, but it was too heavy. "You-all catch hold and pull, too," I suggested. "All together maybe we can do it."

"Need any help?" we heard a voice say. We had been concentrating too hard on the stone to notice him coming up. It was Arie, of course. He sounded real nice and friendly, not sarcastic, now. Well, he ought to, after we had rescued him from that murderer and robber who'd kidnapped him. And now he didn't have any reason to want us not to dig.

We held a quick meeting right there to see if we

could take him back into the Fine-Brain Club, and got all Ayes. After all, he'd had a real good reason for backing out before. And we did need some help with that big rock.

"We voted you back into the Club," I said. "If you want—"

"All right." He scrambled down into the creek bed, to join us.

"The password is Gold," Jenny said. "And it's under this good old Indian rock!"

"How do you know?"

"My sister read it in an Indian book and then looked it up in the dictionary. This is the kind of stone the Indians got their war paint from, so it's got to be the one Colonel Winslow meant."

"Well, it hasn't actually got to," I told her. "Don't be disappointed if it isn't. I just have a kind of feeling that it is. Maybe because I want so much for it to be. It might be what they call woman's intuition, or it might be only what Mama calls wishful thinking. It's not really very smart to count on it."

"I will too be disappointed if it isn't," Jenny said, "because I'm wishful-thinking, too."

"Well, there's just one way to find out," Arie said, and he took the pick and dug it in.

"Hurry," Chuck said. He jumped out of the way when Arie yanked the big stone aside and began to dig underneath it.

We could hardly stand the suspense. It was just like a play. We were all shivering with the excitement and the cold, standing there on the edge of the deepening hole yelping like puppies at every blow of the pick and then holding our breath for the next one. The Indian-red sun came up and the glow touched our faces, and the red rays reached right down into the hole. They shone on the round dirty-looking pieces of metal that fell away from the clay sticking on the pickax—Arie had struck right through the rotten old rusty box and ragged bag the coins were in.

You could see they were gold, under the tarnish.

"Whee! It's really the gold!"

"Gee Wiggles! Gold!"

"This is even better," Arie admitted, lifting the rotting sack out carefully in his hands. "That coin collection musta been valuable, all right, but there sure wasn't much of it. Only fifty-nine coins in the box! I thought sure he musta done something else with part of it, but they said that was all. And ever' one of them little bitty coins was worth about a thousand dollars. Because they're so scarce, the sheriff said. I'm glad these here ain't quite as scarce. There's a lot more of 'em—"

"But they might be collector's items, too, by now," I said, examining one. "English sovereigns, I bet. Go on digging, Arie. There should be another sack and a money belt—that's what Colonel Winslow wrote." The metal box that had contained them had rusted out; it

wasn't fixed up to last under water like the one Bynum Watson used for the rare coins.

Jenny and Chuck started rubbing the gold coins on their sleeves to shine them up a little while Arie and I scrabbled in the clay and rocks with our hands and found the rest. It was just what Colonel Winslow had written: two shot bags and a money belt. But they had rotted too, and the money had spilled out.

"Now Mrs. Beadle can fix up the castle, if she wants to," Jenny said happily.

"But I bet she'd rather use the money to bring her son home from the mental hospital," I said. "Sometimes a patient gets over being dangerous and could come home if there was anyone to take care of him. She could hire somebody good if she had all that money. I hope the government lets her keep it."

"The government don't have to know a thing about it," Arie said. "We don't have to tell 'em."

"Oh, but they will," I told him. "Nobody is supposed to own gold nowadays. She'll have to turn it in at a bank and get paper money for it, if they let her keep it."

"Ain't that a shame," Arie said sympathetically. I felt regretful about the gold, too. Gold is beautiful, because you know when the tarnish comes off it'll have that soft shine. It's no fun to handle paper money. But it's fun to spend it, all right.

We sat cross-legged on the rocks and just looked at the sovereigns for a while. There was so much history tied up in the mere fact that this money existed—it took your breath away to think about it. It was probably part of that loan of gold sovereigns and bullion from England that my history teacher had talked about. The gold had probably run the blockade to get to Richmond! It had been "lost" for nearly a hundred years. And we had found it!

"What do you s'pose became of the rest of the lost Confederate gold?" Jenny said in a hushed voice.

"I wonder," I said. "There was supposed to be half a million dollars, more or less, and some of it was in gold and silver bars, not coins, you know. I think they lost track of it after the Confederacy was dissolved in Washington, Georgia. I believe the history book said only a few thousand dollars—well, maybe it was twenty-five thousand—was captured with President Davis at Irwinville. I guess the officers who had charge of the rest of it might have hidden it and then got killed, like Colonel Winslow did, so that nobody ever knew where to look. The book said people around Washington-Wilkes still dig for it sometimes. Nobody ever accounted for the gold and silver bars. I bet there's plenty of that Confederate treasure still around—but it'll never be found except by accident, or if somebody finds a clue like we did in Colonel Winslow's diary."

I noticed Arie was looking at me kind of funny while I was explaining all this. But I have to tell Jenny and Chuck things they ought to know, because I'm the oldest, and Mama wants us all to be well-informed, she says. I wasn't just showing off. Well, maybe I was, a little. And I was feeling a bit ashamed of it, when Arie said slowly, "I guess books ain't so bad." He didn't have to say any more, but he went on, "Ma says I got to go back to school. Now that we're goin' to get the reward for findin' the college's gold collection, she says we'll be able to move to the old Roberts place and have electric lights and all. Maybe even a washin' machine and a refrigerator. And Ma said she wished Pa could know the college got the scarce old coins back, and she's goin' to take back his name and be Mrs. J. D. Chance again, because she ain't ashamed no more. She believes me now about hearin' him say he wasn't in on stealin' 'em." I imagined them sitting up the rest of that night, just about, making plans and talking about it, and it nearly made me cry.

"And Ma says," Arie went on, "there'll be enough money so I won't need to quit school, and she wants me to finish so I can get a better job than the one in the shoe factory when I graduate. I can work after school now, of course, and Mr. Jenkins thinks he knows where he can get me a part-time job. But Ma says if we want to amount to anything we got to go to school."

"You don't really mind, do you?"

"Naw, I guess not. Things you learn in books—like all this stuff about a long time ago—well, I never thought much about it before. *Now* was about all I could handle. But you kids showed me how things in books are some good, after all. Becky knows so much that I never heard of. Why, I never even knowed about this here money bein' lost."

"Well, you would've, I bet, if you'd listened to your history teacher," I said. "You were probably playing hooky the day they studied about it. You were probably out trapping rabbits." Then I was sorry, because I had sounded as if I thought he was ignorant—and he really wasn't, about a lot of things. "But you know lots more then we do about practical stuff," I said. "I never knew about poke salad until you told me. Nor eating dandelions. Nor purple dye from joe-pye-weed, and all those things. I bet my history teacher couldn't make a rabbit trap that would catch a rabbit!" I began to giggle, imagining Miss Wayne catching rabbits, and then we all giggled and laughed and carried on, because it was so much fun to be alive at sunrise and outdoors, and to have actually found the gold! And because Mrs. Beadle would be so astonished and happy when we took it to her.

She was, too. We had to take it back to the cabin first, of course, to show Sarge and Grandma, and it sure felt funny to have our pockets full of gold pieces. We had to tie the rest of it up in my sweater, like a bag. And we nearly died laughing at the expression on Sarge's and Grandma's faces, when we dumped it all out on the table and told them what we had really been digging for. Grandma said you could have knocked her over with a feather. Chuck tried it, but he couldn't. Sarge said maybe he didn't use a big enough feather.

They let us take Sarge's canvas Army bag to carry the money over to Wormwood in. Mrs. Beadle said, "Bless you," and she had tears in her eyes, and she didn't call Jenny her Nellie at all. And she said she was glad to meet Arie, and that he could set his rabbit traps anywhere he wanted to on her property.

She was glad to meet Sarge and Grandma, too. They had come with us. With all that gold, I guess they must've been afraid somebody would rob us on the way over. It was almost like having a party at Wormwood.

We were dying to know what Mrs. Beadle would do with the money when the bank changed it for her. Sarge said he didn't think the United States Government would be heartless enough to take it from her even if they did have a right to confiscate it. After all, her own grandfather put it there, and the land had been hers before the lake was there. As for treasure-trove belonging to whoever found it, we would certainly waive any claim we might have, because we knew it belonged to Mrs. Beadle. Sarge said she could probably get a lot of money for that little book, too, from some collector of authentic Confederate items—if she wanted to sell it.

We wished she would get somebody to finish building the castle, the way old Jefferey—Geoffrey—wanted it to be, but we knew she wouldn't. My guess was right

—I had guessed she would want to have her son home with her so she wouldn't be lonesome any more. She said she had dreamed about being able to do that. "He was a good boy, Dick was," she said. I figured he must be an old man by now, but to her he was still a boy. Her boy. She'd saved those baby shoes . . . "He just needs treatment that he can't get in the state hospital. If I can pay for it—and for a good man to stay here and look after him—"

Sarge told her that he'd heard of a lot of new medical discoveries that might help her son, and he would try to find out what could be done. He warned her not to count on it, but he'd try. Having been in the Army medics, Sarge knows a lot about doctors and hospitals. And he would ask Mr. Carmichael, one of the vice-presidents at the bank in town, to come out and see her about the details of reporting the gold and turning it in for money she could use. If she wanted to see a lawyer, he would get a good one for her.

That meant, of course, that she would be seeing people again. She wouldn't be a lady hermit, any more. She had stayed alone, withdrawn from everybody, so long—you could tell she was having a hard time trying to decide that she could do it. But then Jenny snuggled up to her and said, "You'll like Mr. Carmichael, Mrs. Beadle. He's nice."

Mrs. Beadle said, "Bless you," again to Jenny, and to Sarge, "All right. Thank you very much. I'll see him tomorrow morning. And—thank you, all of you. You are all so kind."

She made Jenny and me promise that we'd come back to see her the next afternoon, and we did. Arie and Chuck, too, though actually I think she likes girls better than boys.

We had already voted, and everybody voted Aye. We were all gathered around her where she sat on the old leather couch, and Jenny said, "We all voted for you to be an honorary member of the Fine-Brain Club, Mrs. Beadle. That's better than an ordinary member because you don't have to do any of the work. And we'll have the meetings here at your house if you want us to, so you can come to them."

She was so surprised she nearly cried. "I certainly do want you to," she said. "Bless you."

We told her the password, which was "Indian Red" that day, and gave her the grip and all. And the secret call. When she tried she could sound almost as much like a bobwhite as Arie could.

Then she told us why she had wanted us to come that afternoon, after she saw Mr. Carmichael. She wanted to give each of us one of the gold English sovereigns for a keepsake, and Mr. Carmichael had said it was all right with the government for gold coins to be kept by coin-collectors, but not to be put in circulation.

So all of us started rare-coin collections right then, and maybe some day we'll have a collection as good as the one Arie got back for the college. Even Arie started his own collection. He said he didn't know a thing about rare coins, but I promised I'd lend him a book about them, just as soon as I got one and read it myself.